THE OTHER AMISH GIRL

(The Miracle Creek Amish Romances, Book 4)

GRACE SPRINGFIELD

ISBN 978-1-918219-45-6

First Edition: 2025
Published by: Cosmic Jive Publishing

www.cosmicjivepublishing.com

For permissions and inquiries, contact:
info@cosmicjivepublishing.com

Disclaimer:

This is a work of fiction. Names, characters, businesses, places, events, locales, and incidents are either the products of the author's imagination or used in a fictitious manner. Any resemblance to actual persons, living or dead, or actual events is purely coincidental.

Chapter 1
A Quiet Longing

The needle pierced the fabric with quiet precision, each stitch a meditation. Esther Troyer sat at her wooden sewing table, candlelight casting amber shadows across the blue and green squares taking shape beneath her fingers. Outside the modest farmhouse windows, Lancaster County stretched in golden waves under the afternoon sun, but Esther's thoughts had drifted somewhere beyond the careful seams—to a longing she couldn't quite name, a restlessness that hummed beneath her practiced calm.

The sewing table occupied a corner of the main room where white-painted walls held the day's light. The furnishings were spare—an unadorned bench, her father's reading chair worn smooth by years of evening Bible study. Every night the candles flickered like heartbeats, and today was no different, flames dancing across her work with the rhythm of something alive.

Her hands moved without thought now, muscle memory guiding each pull of thread. The quilt emerging beneath her fingers was both duty and desire—the traditional patterns her mother had taught her, yes, but also something more. The interplay of blue and green reminded her of Miracle Creek's rolling hills, of wildflowers bursting through spring grass, of sky meeting earth at the horizon.

Esther's gaze drifted to the window. Children's silhouettes flickered near the barn, their laughter floating through the glass like birdsong. Something in her chest tightened—a bittersweet ache for futures she couldn't quite envision, for a life that felt perpetually just out of reach. Would her hands ever stitch together more than fabric?

Would she ever piece together the fragments of a shared life, two hearts instead of one?

The thimble's soft click faltered. Her needle hung suspended mid-stitch as her focus scattered like dandelion seeds on wind. She'd been daydreaming again—about distant places, unexplored adventures, and most dangerously, about love. The kind of love that seemed to belong to other people, not to Esther Troyer who sat alone at her sewing table year after year. She was only twenty-three, but at times she felt she led her life as if she were forty-three.

With a slow exhale, she forced her attention back to the quilt. The blue reminded her of possibility, of skies that went on forever. Each stitch became a tiny prayer, a wish sewn into cotton and thread.

The farmhouse held its familiar sounds around her—floorboards creaking their wooden song, the distant clatter of dishes, the murmur of voices from another room. These were her constants, the framework of her days.

But somewhere beneath the surface, something was shifting. What had begun as simple sewing had become something deeper—a canvas for longing, for dreams that churned quietly in the spaces between stitches. She could feel herself in every pull of thread, capturing hope and heartache in equal measure, weaving them tightly into the emerging pattern. Each stitch sealed her wishes into the fabric itself, fortifying the sense of purpose that lit her from within even as it ached.

As evening light faded toward dusk, Esther paused to admire her progress. The quilt was half-finished but already vibrant with color and life, already beautiful in its becoming. Yet even as she studied her work with satisfaction, that gentle ache settled over her once more— the weight of wanting something more, something beyond these four walls and this solitary table.

With one last lingering glance through the window at the golden fields, Esther returned to her task. The flickering candlelight guided her hands as she pressed onward, lost in the swirl of blue and green that felt so much like the threads of her own restless heart.

* * *

The steady clip-clop of hooves on packed dirt created a rhythm that matched Esther's heartbeat as she sat beside her father in the buggy. Crisp autumn air filled her lungs with each breath, carrying the scent of harvest and woodsmoke. They were headed to the community barn for the Singing, and the anticipation built with every turn of the wheels—a mixture of nerves and excitement that made her acutely aware of every sensation, every sound.

Daniel Troyer held the reins with steady hands, his weathered face composed in its usual expression of quiet authority. The brown fabric of his trousers brushed against Esther's dress as the buggy swayed, grounding her even as her thoughts spiraled ahead to the evening's possibilities.

Beside her, Mae's cheerful chatter filled the space between them like birdsong. "Can you believe we're finally going? I heard they've been practicing all week!" Her younger sister's enthusiasm was infectious, pulling at the corners of Esther's mouth despite the nervous flutter in her stomach.

"*Ja*," Esther managed, her smile soft and genuine. "It should be a wonderful evening."

"Indeed it should," Daniel agreed, glancing at Esther with eyes that saw perhaps more than she wanted to reveal. But he said nothing about the tension in her posture, the way her hands twisted in her lap.

Mae continued her torrent of excitement, recounting everything she'd heard about who would perform and what songs they'd sing. Esther let the words wash over her, focusing instead on the approaching barn—a rustic silhouette against the setting sun that seemed to pulse with gathered life.

As they drew closer, the barn grew more distinct. Lamplight glowed through the open doors, and the sound of voices and laughter drifted across the fields like an invitation. Colors bloomed in the doorway—the deep blues and greens and burgundies of Sunday best, the white of prayer *kapps*, the varied shades of beards and suspenders. The community gathering, all in one place, all together.

The familiar sounds wrapped around Esther as they arrived—greetings called out, conversations overlapping, the shuffle of feet and rustle of fabric.

Something stirred in her chest, equal parts anticipation and dread. Would her heart remain forever silent? Always watching, never participating in her own story?

They climbed down from the buggy, shoes crunching on dirt and gravel. Mae grabbed Esther's hand, tugging her toward the barn with barely contained excitement. Inside, wooden benches had been arranged in neat rows, and the air already hummed with melody—voices warming up, someone testing a pitch.

And then Esther's eyes found him.

Eli Yoder stood among a cluster of young men near the far wall, tall and solid against the backdrop of hay bales and candlelight. A laugh erupted from him—hearty and genuine—his broad shoulders shaking with mirth. The light caught on his dark beard, illuminating the strong lines of his face, and for a moment the bustling barn faded to nothing. Time itself seemed to pause.

Esther drew in a sharp breath. The world had narrowed to just him, just that laugh, just the way the light loved the planes of his face.

But he wasn't alone.

Martha Stoltzfus stood at his elbow, bright-eyed and radiant as always. They were sharing some joke, laughter passing between them as easily as breathing, and Esther felt something crack open in her chest—a fragile, fluttering thing taking flight even as it broke.

Her stomach twisted as she watched them. Martha was everything Esther wasn't—confident, outgoing, always knowing exactly what to say and when to say it. And Eli... Eli looked at Martha with an ease that made Esther's throat tight with longing and resignation in equal measure.

What Esther didn't know—what she couldn't know as she stood there clutching her shawl—was that five years earlier, Eli Yoder had stood outside her family's kitchen window with his heart hammering against his ribs. He'd spent weeks gathering courage, had picked wildflowers like a fool, had rehearsed the words he would say to her father when asking permission to court her.

He'd been so certain. The way Esther's eyes had lit up when they'd talked at the last barn raising, the gentle brush of her hand against his when she'd passed him tools—it had all meant something, hadn't it?

But before he could knock, voices had drifted through the open window. Mae's teasing tone had been unmistakable: "Esther's sweet on Eli Yoder, isn't she?"

And then Esther's response, sharp and immediate, had pierced straight through him: "Don't be ridiculous, Mae. Eli Yoder and me? I have no interest in him that way. None at all."

He'd stood frozen, the bunch of wildflowers wilting in his suddenly nerveless fingers. The embarrassment in her tone had been clear—as if the very suggestion was absurd, almost offensive. He'd stumbled away from that window with his carefully rehearsed words dying on his lips and his heart cracking like ice on a warming creek.

What Eli hadn't known—what he couldn't have known —was that the much younger and less mature Esther had been burning with mortification at her sister's teasing. She'd denied her feelings out of pure embarrassment, terrified that someone might overhear and spread gossip through the community. Her denial had been self-protection, not truth.

But Eli had believed every word.

So sometime later when Martha Stoltzfus had smiled at him at Sunday service, when she'd asked about his farm with genuine interest, when she'd made it clear without being forward that she would welcome his attention—he'd tried. Bit by bit he'd tried. He'd tried to redirect his wounded heart toward someone who actually wanted him.

Their courtship had been the talk of the community for weeks now. Proper, respectable, exactly what everyone expected. Folks had even begun discussing a betrothal—an arrangement of convenience and expectation more than mutual passion, some said, but practical nonetheless.

Yet even now, as Esther watched from across the barn, she couldn't know that every time Eli laughed at Martha's jokes, he was thinking of Esther's quiet smile. Every time Martha's hand brushed his arm, he remembered the way Esther's fingers had trembled when she'd handed him that cup of water at the summer work frolic. Every time he told himself he was content, a voice whispered liar.

"Ten years of watching him," Mae whispered, nudging Esther's elbow with a mischievous grin, "and still not a word from you to him."

Heat flooded Esther's cheeks. She quickly dropped her

gaze, but not before Mae caught the expression on her face.

"Awwie, Mae!" Esther hissed, urgency making her voice sharp.

"I'm only saying what my eyes see!" Mae chuckled, the sound rich with sisterly knowing. Esther felt the weight of her longing like a physical thing, wrapped tight as a hidden seam, as carefully concealed as her finest stitches.

The community began to gather for the singing, voices rising in harmonious unison. Esther's heart raced with every stolen glance at Eli—her spirit soaring and plummeting with each note, each harmony echoing against the wood-beamed structure. His laughter lingered in her thoughts like a song she couldn't stop humming, teasing her with possibility even as reality held her fast.

And yet, despite the gathering and the camaraderie and the blending of voices, Esther remained an outsider to her own story. Always observing. Always yearning for the moment when she might finally speak the words dancing on the tip of her tongue. But here, within the community's embrace, where love for music intertwined seamlessly with love of family and friends, she kept her heart close— hidden within her careful stitches of longing.

* * *

After the singing concluded, the community spilled outside into the golden evening light. Esther stood at the edge of the yard, caught between the joyous energy of her family and the tightening knot in her chest as she watched Eli help Martha into his buggy. The sun glinted off the dark strands of his beard, catching on the buttons of his shirt, making everything seem to glow.

She moved to assist her father, who was already at their

buggy arranging the baskets and blankets they'd brought. The familiar duties provided welcome distraction, but each movement felt heavy with unspoken words. Her fingers brushed the textured surfaces of the woven baskets—a subtle reminder of her bond with family, even as her heart remained elsewhere.

"Make sure it's balanced, Esther," Daniel instructed, his voice steady amid the flutter of departing families.

She nodded, but her mind was only partially present. Her eyes were drawn again and again to where Eli stood, his sturdy form unmistakable even in the throng of people.

Martha's laughter bubbled like water over stones—sweet and uncomplicated, clinging to the air around them. As Eli helped her into the buggy, the tenderness of his actions resonated deep in Esther's chest. There was an ease in his gestures, a familiarity that made her stomach twist. His hand rested gently on the small of Martha's back—a touch that felt intimate and right in a world that felt all wrong for Esther.

"Esther, *mei dochder,*" Daniel called, breaking through her reverie as he noticed her distant gaze. "Can you bring over that last blanket?"

His presence anchored her, pulling her back to the moment. She complied, forcing herself to suppress the ache building within.

Yet her heart remained unanchored. She caught snippets of conversations—plans for the week ahead, laughter about something that had happened during the singing—but all Esther could see was Eli with Martha, the way he made the other girl's smile shine with an intensity that highlighted her every feature.

Esther helped her father load the buggy, arranging the blankets with meticulous care, yet her gaze continually flickered back to Eli. The longing deepened each time she caught him smiling at Martha.

Then, a moment arose.

Eli turned, and their eyes locked across the distance. Time slowed to honey-thick. The world dissolved around them, reality drawing taut like thread pulled tight. Esther felt her breath hitch. In that instant, something whispered between them—a fleeting connection laden with possibility, with the ghost of what might have been.

But it slipped away as quickly as it arrived. His gaze slid back to Martha, uncertainty flickering in his eyes before he turned away fully. The warm bubble of possibility broke, leaving Esther cold in its absence.

"Esther," Daniel called again, and she turned reluctantly toward her father, blinking against the light as if waking from a dream.

"Let's finish up, *dochder*. The day's drawing to a close."

His voice commanded respect, and she nodded. The softness in her heart wrestled with duty as she climbed into the buggy beside her father. The seat felt familiar yet heavier now, burdened by longing that settled in the pit of her stomach.

As they set off down the path, she could feel Eli's gaze upon her once more—or perhaps it was only her imagination, her desperate heart conjuring connection where there was only distance and misunderstanding.

* * *

That night, after her family had retired and the house settled into stillness, Esther knelt beside her bed in flickering candlelight. Her hands clasped together so tightly her knuckles showed white.

"Dear Lord," she whispered into the darkness, "I know it is not my place to question Your will, but this loneliness...

it weighs so heavy on my heart."

Her voice cracked. Tears slipped down her cheeks.

"If Eli is not meant for me, please... please take away this ache. Or if there is to be someone else, someone You have planned for me, make a way. You parted the Red Sea for Your people. Surely You can make a way for one lost heart?"

She thought of the Scripture her mother had loved: *Trust in the Lord with all thine heart; and lean not unto thine own understanding.*

"I am trying to trust," Esther breathed. "I am trying to understand. But it is so very hard, *Gott.*"

The candle guttered, casting dancing shadows on the wall. Esther remained on her knees until they ached, pouring out her heart to the only One who could truly hear it.

Outside, the stars wheeled overhead—silent witnesses to a love story tangled in misunderstanding. Two hearts yearning for each other, each believing the other felt nothing at all.

Chapter 2
Whispers and Shadows

As the afternoon light filtered through the plain curtains of Miriam Albrecht's low-ceilinged home, Esther settled into the familiar rhythm of the quilting circle. The gentle click of needles intertwined with whispers of fabric being rearranged, a symphony of industry and camaraderie that echoed through the modest space.

Around her, the room buzzed with the chatter of women nestled close together, their laughter mingling seamlessly with the fabric that shifted beneath their busy hands. The low hum of conversation enveloped Esther like a comforting blanket, yet something deeper crept beneath the surface, coiling tight in her chest.

She focused intently on her work, her needle darting through the blue and green fabric as it became something more than just patches stitched together. It was an act of creation, a quilt imbued with love and care, each strand weaving stories that perhaps had been told a thousand times over. But today, her thoughts danced at the fringes of her concentration, lured in by the soft whispers filtering from across the circle.

"Veronica, did you see Martha Stoltzfus this past market day?" Mary Beiler leaned closer, the sharp creak of the chair echoing in the small room.

Esther's fingers trembled for a fleeting moment, the needle hovering just above the quilt as she struggled to rein in her curiosity.

"Indeed, I did," Veronica Zook replied, her voice barely rising above the rustling fabric. "I heard from Mammi Yoder herself—the arrangement between Martha and Eli is finalized."

Esther felt her heart quicken, a rapid staccato echoing within her chest as she fought to remain focused on her stitching. She allowed herself to steal glances at the women, their faces illuminated with the thrill of shared information. Each glance revealed a world of knowing smirks and raised eyebrows, the way they exchanged glances filled with both curiosity and judgment.

"It's not a love match, you understand," Dorcas Hershberger added, her needle pausing mid-stitch. "More of a practical arrangement. The Yoder farm borders the Stoltzfus property, and you know how these things are decided."

"Still," Emma Albrecht said with a sigh, "Martha seems pleased enough with the arrangement. I'd say she's glowing. And Eli... well, he's doing his duty."

Esther's fingers stilled mid-stitch, the weight of her needle pressing against the fabric, a reminder of the heaviness in her own heart. The others remained enraptured, oblivious to the tempest their words stirred within her.

Veronica leaned in closer, her voice dropping to barely above a whisper as she appeared to stare right at Esther. "Though I did notice something peculiar at the last singing. Did you see the way Eli looked across the barn? His eyes weren't on Martha at all."

Esther's pulse quickened further, panic creeping at the edges of her resolve. She forced herself to keep stitching, to maintain the steady rhythm that might hide the trembling in her hands.

She felt Veronica Zook's eyes bore through her in what seemed like an interminable silence that followed.

"Oh, don't start with your romantic notions," Dorcas chided gently, breaking the silence. "The arrangement is all but settled. What does it matter where his eyes wander? Duty is duty."

The words struck Esther like stones. Duty. Arrangement. Settled. Each word fell heavy, suffocating the small flame of hope she'd been nursing in secret.

Esther shifted in her seat, the fabric beneath her fingers feeling foreign, the rhythm she had found disrupted. It was not merely gossip that shook her core; it was the gnawing reminder of her own dreams left unvoiced.

"Do you think Martha will move to the Yoder farm after the wedding?" Emma mused. "It would make sense, with Mammi Yoder needing care and all."

"I heard the wedding might be as soon as late autumn," Veronica added. "Before the hard winter sets in. These arrangements don't usually drag on once things have agreed."

Esther felt her breath hitch, her chest tightening with each word. Late autumn. That was just a couple of months away. The weight of lost time pressed down upon her shoulders like a physical burden.

She remembered the way Eli had looked at her that evening after the singing—that moment when their eyes had met across the yard. There had been something there, hadn't there? Or had it been merely her imagination, her desperate heart conjuring connection where none existed?

Then she recalled Dorcas' words from just moments before. It did not matter where his eyes wandered. If the betrothal was arranged, if it was about land and duty and practical matters... then perhaps Eli had no more choice in this than she had voice to speak against it.

"Esther, dear, you've gone quite pale," Miriam Albrecht said suddenly. "Are you feeling well?"

The room fell silent, all eyes turning to Esther. She felt heat flood her cheeks as she realized she'd been sitting motionless, her needle suspended in air, her face surely betraying the tumult within.

Widow Kauffman's weathered hand reached across to rest on Esther's arm, the touch gentle, reassuring. Her eyes were warm, full of a quiet understanding that needed no words. *You don't have to explain,* they seemed to say. *I know. I, too, have loved and lost. I, too, have ached for someone I could not have. We are not so different, you and I.*

She smiled then, a small, knowing curve of the lips, and gave Esther's arm a soft, comforting pat.

"I—*ja,* I'm fine," Esther managed, forcing her needle back into motion. "*Denki* for asking. Just concentrating on this difficult pattern."

But Miriam's knowing eyes lingered on her face a moment longer than comfortable, and Esther had the unsettling feeling that the older woman saw far more than Esther wished to reveal.

Veronica's face was a portrait of quiet satisfaction. Dorcas smirked, then quickly rearranged it into something resembling a pious smile. Another little morsel to whisper about later.

As the conversation gradually resumed around her, Esther's mind spun with memories and regrets. She thought of all the times over the years when she might have spoken, might have been brave. The summer work frolic when Eli had lingered near her, making excuses to talk about nothing in particular. The singing five years ago when he'd asked to drive her home, and she'd been too nervous to accept, making up an excuse about riding with her family.

"Some things are simply not meant to be," Dorcas was saying now, her voice carrying the weight of resignation and acceptance that defined their way of life.

Widow Kauffman cleared her throat—loudly, pointedly

—just shy of outright disagreement. And then, as if to confirm Emma's suspicions, she shot Emma a quick, conspiratorial wink when no one else was looking, before lifting her glass and taking an exaggerated sip of water. A spark lit the old woman's eyes—fire, mischief, or something in between. Emma couldn't quite tell.

"We must trust in *Gott's* plan and the wisdom of our elders." Dorcas continued.

Esther nodded along with the others, her needle moving in steady rhythm once more, but inside, her heart cried out in silent protest. Was this truly *Gott's* plan? Or was it merely the consequence of two hearts now forever kept apart by fear and propriety?

She kept her gaze fixed on her stitching, refusing to meet Widow Kauffman's eyes again. Hope was a cruel thing—sweet at first, then sharp enough to wound. The widow's wink had been a tiny invitation, a fragile opening, and Esther knew better than to take it. Hope only led to disappointment.

Hope hurt.

As the afternoon light shifted and stretched, casting long shadows across the quilting frame, Esther made a decision. She would attend the harvest gathering next week. She would see Eli and Martha together for more than a few moments—would witness this new arrangement with her own eyes. Maybe then, faced with the truth of it, her heart would finally accept what her mind already knew: that Eli Yoder was not meant for her, and she must find a way to let him go once and for all.

But even as she made this resolution, stitching it into her heart as firmly as she stitched the pattern into her quilt, a small, stubborn voice whispered in the depths of her soul: *But what if? What if there's still time? What if he needs only to know the truth of how she felt? Plans, even well-meaning ones, aren't always written in stone—not even among the Amish.* The thought sent heat rushing to her cheeks. She recalled the part of Scripture where *Gott* parted the Red Sea for His people, and the memory made her blush all the more—at her own boldness, at the hope flickering inside her, a spark fanned to life by Widow Kauffman's wink. Or had it been there all along, waiting for the smallest breath to stir it back to flame?

The women around her continued their work and their talk, the quilting circle spinning out its comfortable rhythms, while Esther sat among them—present in body but adrift in spirit, caught between resignation and a hope she dared not name aloud.

* * *

The scent of ripe apples and fragrant cinnamon filled the air, wrapping around the community harvest gathering like an inviting embrace. Esther stood at the long wooden table lined with jars of preserves, the vibrant colors glistening in the gentle autumn light. The festival thrummed with life, laughter intermingling with the warm notes of conversation, yet amidst the celebration, her heart felt heavy.

Families strolled from one display to another, eager to showcase the bounty of their harvests. Children darted between the adults, their delighted squeals punctuating the steady hum of activity. The wooden apple press groaned rhythmically as men took turns cranking the handle, golden cider flowing into waiting buckets.

Nearby, the scent of Emma Albrecht's new orange-and-lemon cookies drifted through the air, drawing a steadily growing line of neighbors curious to taste her latest creation. Laughter rose from the group gathered around her table, the bright citrus aroma mingling with the earthier scents of autumn.

Esther set out her family's preserves with careful hands, arranging each jar so the sunlight would catch the deep jewel tones of berry, apple and peach. The gentle bustle around her should have been comforting, but her thoughts kept drifting—unwelcome, insistent—back to Eli. As she worked, her gaze kept drifting toward the clearing where the apple pressing station sat, where Eli Yoder stood among a group of men, his broad shoulders outlined against the autumn sky.

"Esther, these preserves are beautiful," Miriam Albrecht said warmly, pausing to admire the display. "Your mother's recipe?"

"*Ja,*" Esther replied softly, managing a smile. "*Mamm* taught me to add just a touch of vanilla to the apple butter. It makes all the difference."

As Anna moved on, Esther's attention was drawn once more to the pressing station. Martha Stoltzfus stood nearby, her burgundy dress crisp and unwrinkled beneath her apron, laughing at something one of the older women had said. She looked perfectly comfortable, perfectly at ease in her role as Eli's intended.

But as Esther watched, she noticed something that made her breath catch. Eli's posture was tense, his movements mechanical as he worked the apple press. Even from this distance, she could see the tightness around his mouth, the way his jaw clenched when Martha approached him.

And then Martha was at his side, her hand touching his arm in what should have been a familiar, affectionate gesture. But Eli stiffened—just slightly, just enough that Esther's trained eye caught it. He didn't pull away, but neither did he lean into the touch. He merely continued working, his responses to Martha's conversation brief and measured.

Esther's heart twisted with an emotion she couldn't quite name. Was it hope? Sympathy? Or simply the pain of watching someone she loved trapped in the same cage of duty and expectation that confined her?

"Quite a picture they make, don't they?" Mae appeared at Esther's elbow, her voice carefully neutral. "Though if you ask me, Eli looks about as happy as a horse being led to auction."

"Mae," Esther whispered urgently, glancing around to make sure no one had overheard. "You shouldn't say such things."

"Why not, when it's true?" Mae's young face was unusually serious. Just two years her junior, Mae seemed often a world apart in her thinking. "Everyone pretends not to notice, but I've been watching. He's going through the motions, Esther. Nothing more."

Before Esther could respond, a commotion near the pressing station drew their attention. Martha had said something—her voice hadn't carried, but her expression had shifted from pleasant to confused. Eli had turned away slightly, his hand running through his dark hair in what looked like frustration.

The older women nearby exchanged glances, their conversation faltering. Veronica's eyes narrowed. A tongue darted across Dorcas Herhsberger's lips as if she was already practicing the tittle tattle about this scene for later. The blacksmith, John Hostetler, who had been helping at the press, placed a steadying hand on Eli's shoulder and spoke quietly to him. Whatever John said seemed to calm the younger man, though the tension didn't leave his frame.

Martha stepped back, her smile now fixed and brittle. She smoothed her apron with quick, agitated movements, then excused herself and walked toward the women's gathering area, her cheeks flushed.

Esther's heart ached for all of them—for Eli, clearly struggling with the weight of his obligations; for Martha, who surely sensed she was not truly wanted; and for herself, watching it all from a distance, powerless to change anything.

Meanwhile, Widow Kauffman sat leaning on her cane, her face a picture of keen observation wrapped in innocent curiosity. Her eyes missed nothing. Every shift in posture, every strained smile, every glance that lingered too long— she absorbed it all with the quiet, knowing look of someone who had lived long enough to recognize the truths people tried to hide.

Widow Kauffman's gaze drifted back to Esther, settling on her with quiet insistence. It was as though she were urging her to act, urging her to *believe*. As if her very eyes were saying, *It's all right to hope, child. It's all right to want more than what you've been handed.*

"I should bring some cider to the workers," Esther said suddenly, to nobody in particular, grateful for an excuse to move, to do something other than stand and observe.

She filled a pitcher with fresh-pressed cider and gathered several cups on a tray, her hands steady despite the racing of her heart. As she approached the pressing station, she saw her father notice her coming and nod approvingly—offering refreshment was expected, proper, exactly what a good *dochder* should do.

But as she neared, Eli turned, and their eyes met.

The world seemed to slow. In that moment, Esther saw past the dutiful farmer, past the obedient son fulfilling his family's unspoken wishes. She saw the boy who had once shared her lunch when he'd forgotten his at school. She saw the young man who had looked at her after the singing with something that might have been longing. She saw someone as trapped as she was, bound by expectations.

"You must be thirsty after all the work today," she said gently, her voice barely above a whisper as she extended a cup of cider toward him.

For a heartbeat, Eli simply looked at her, and in his eyes Esther saw something that made her breath catch—recognition, regret, and something deeper that she didn't dare name.

Then, as if remembering himself, he turned away abruptly, his jaw tightening. "I'm fine," he said gruffly, the words clipped and distant.

The rejection stung like a physical blow. Esther's hand trembled slightly, the cup still extended between them, an offering refused. She felt heat rise to her cheeks as awareness of the watching eyes around them prickled along her skin. Heat rushed to her cheeks as she became all too aware of the watching eyes around them, each one a silent witness to her misstep. Foolish. That's how she felt. Foolish for listening to Widow Kauffman. Foolish for daring to follow her heart.

What she didn't know—what she couldn't possibly know—was that Eli's heart was hammering in his chest. Every fiber of him longed to take that cup, to let his fingers brush hers, to tell her he'd heard her words that day five years ago… and to ask if he had misunderstood them. *Could* they have changed? Five years was a long time. A long time to love someone he believed did not love him back. And yet his heart had never let Esther go.

But he hadn't taken the cup—because Martha was somewhere nearby. He had no desire to hurt her. She was *gut* to him, he supposed. Their betrothal was all but set in stone; Martha had been gently nudging him toward commitment for months, each hesitant retreat on his part only strengthening her resolve. She'd been subtle, yes—but Amish women had their ways. He had delayed, unsure, but he could grow to love Martha in time, he guessed. Many did. His own parents had.

And then there was his pride—the old wound of Esther's refusal still hot in his chest. Even now, as he found himself wondering whether she had spoken those words to her sister out of embarrassment. *What if* she hadn't meant them? *What if* she'd felt something for him after all?

But just as quickly came the other side of the blade: *What if* she had meant them—every syllable—and he was a fool for hoping otherwise?

But it didn't matter now. He had made his choice. He had committed himself to this path. He was trying to be a man and stoic but his words to Esther had a much sharper tone than intended.

"Suit yourself," Esther said quietly, her voice admirably steady as she turned toward the other workers. But Eli saw the hurt flash across her face, saw the way her shoulders curved inward slightly as if protecting herself from another blow.

He watched her move away, offering cider to the other men, her gentle smile in place, her manner gracious and kind. Every step she took away from him felt like a loss he had no right to mourn.

John Hostetler approached him again, this time with a question in his eyes.

"That was unlike you, Eli," he said quietly. "Esther meant only kindness."

"I know," Eli managed, gripping the apple press handle tighter than necessary. "I know."

But knowing and doing were two different things. How could he accept her kindness when every interaction with her stirred up the longing he'd tried so hard to bury? How could he stand close to her and not confess everything—the overheard conversation, his wounded pride, the betrothal that felt more like a noose with each passing day?

John Hostetler looked as if he were about to speak, then thought better of it. His gaze shifted to Esther for a moment before settling back on Eli, a silent question hanging in his eyes—unspoken, yet impossible to miss.

Esther returned to her family's table, where her father now stood with Bishop Samuel Lapp, both men watching the gathering with the measured assessment of leaders weighing the health of their community. She saw them exchange looks as they observed the scene that had just unfolded—small gestures, subtle tensions, the complex web of relationships that made up their world.

"Some choices are harder than others," she heard the bishop say to her father, though his words seemed directed at no one in particular. "But we must trust that *Gott* works all things together for *gut*."

Esther wanted to believe that. She wanted to trust that this painful tangle of misunderstanding and duty would somehow work itself into a pattern that made sense. But as she watched Eli return to his work, his movements jerky with suppressed emotion, and saw Martha approach him again with renewed determination, Esther felt hope slipping through her fingers like water through a sieve.

The harvest gathering continued around them, the celebration of abundance and community carrying on despite the quiet heartbreak unfolding in its midst. Emma Albrecht's tempting cookies sold out quickly. Life went on, as it always did, indifferent to the silent struggles of two hearts that had never learned how to speak their truth aloud.

As the afternoon light began to slant golden and long, Esther helped her family pack their goods, loading jars carefully into wooden crates. She moved with practiced efficiency, but her mind was miles away, replaying that moment when Eli had abruptly turned his attentions from her, wondering why and what she might have done differently.

The echoes of the harvest gathering etched themselves deeply into her soul, marking the turning of a page she was yet unready to face but needed to navigate in her quest for belonging and love. And as their buggy rolled away from the festivities, Esther turned back one last time to see Eli standing alone near the apple press, watching their departure with an expression she couldn't quite read—but that her heart insisted meant something, even if she couldn't let herself believe it.

Silently, she whispered in her heart just four words. *Lord, make a way.*

Chapter 3
A Helping Hand

The sweet, yeasty aroma of rising bread enveloped Esther like a warm embrace, the sunlight pouring through the window illuminating the fine dusting of flour that clung to her apron. Each rhythmic knead of the dough felt grounding, an anchor against the swirling thoughts of longing and unease that had taken root within her. The kitchen hummed with familiarity, yet beneath the surface, a quiet anxiety lingered.

As she pressed her palms down into the pliable dough, she thought of her mother and the way they had once baked together, laughter echoing around the kitchen as flour dusted their cheeks like winter snow. The wooden table felt sturdy beneath Esther, a testament to generations of her family, just like the recipe she used—a steadfast guide passed through whispered stories. A smile danced on her lips as she remembered her mother's advice, *"Gut bread is made with a soft heart and gentle hands,"* a reminder that sometimes, creation and care could bloom within the confines of domesticity.

Yet, amidst the warmth, the silence shattered as the door creaked open, and Deborah Peachey hurried in. Her cheeks were flushed, their redness almost as red as her hair, breath coming in quick bursts. The usual serene air of the kitchen grew heavy with urgency.

"Esther!" Deborah called, the edges of her voice laced with panic.

Esther dropped the dough back onto the floured surface, wiping her hands on her apron as she turned. "Deborah, ach, what on earth is wrong?"

"It's Mammi Yoder," Deborah exclaimed, urgency

causing the young woman to clasp her hands tightly. "She's taken ill—pneumonia, I believe. But the *doktor* and his wife are away visiting Tall Poplars for another three days at least."

"*Ach, mei hart—pneumonia?*" Esther whispered.

Each word had struck Esther like a hammer, sending a flare of worry through her chest. Eli's grandmother—who had cared for him since his parents had passed, one to cancer, the other to a broken heart, as some whispered—was usually the very embodiment of warmth and wisdom. The thought of the sweet, fragile matriarch gravely ill filled Esther with a wave of dread that twisted in her stomach.

Esther's hands trembled as she listened, instinctively moving to gather her herb basket. "I—I'll help. I know what to do." The knowledge flowed through her veins, learned from the soothing whispers of her mother, memories of herbal remedies mingling with her pulse.

With deliberate movements, Esther collected dried elderberry and yarrow, each sprig she selected a thread binding her to the community, her mother's teachings woven into every choice.

Her heart raced as she filled the basket, adrenaline sharpening her senses while her hands trembled ever so slightly—a reminder of the responsibility looming over her like dark clouds gathering before a storm.

"Gather whatever you need," Deborah urged, a flicker of gratitude brightening her eyes. "I'm not sure what all they have at the farm. The community depends on your skills. I wish I knew what to do—I just feel so helpless, you know..."

The young, capable schoolteacher gave a small, frustrated shrug, clearly unaccustomed to such helplessness. "When Eli came to me asking for medical help, I had to tell him I couldn't do anything for his mother. I said I'd fetch the *doktor* for him, but of course the Matthews are away…" She shook her head. "It was Anne Hostetler—the blacksmith's wife—who told me you know your way around herbs better than anyone else."

Esther nodded, feeling the weight of the words press against her like a vice. The kitchen, once a sanctuary, morphed into a conduit of urgency. She took a moment to close her eyes and breathe, steadying herself before stepping into the world outside where her thoughts of Eli Yoder waited, sharp and unwelcome.

He had filled her mind since that bittersweet moment at the harvest gathering, where his rejection had cut deeper than she cared to admit. Yet now was not the time for her own heartache. Mammi Yoder needed her. And Eli would be there—try as she might, she could not ignore the thought, not even when she forced herself to think of other things.

"Let's go," she said to Deborah, her voice steadier than she felt. "And I can teach you some herbal basics sometime, if you'd like."

With the herb basket tucked securely in her arms and Deborah gushing her thanks at the offer, Esther climbed into the waiting buggy. Each jolt of the wooden wheels felt like a reminder of her own uncertain footing.

The world outside unfurled, the golden fields of Lancaster County stretching wide under a bright, cobalt sky. She watched other Amish farms blink by, laundry swaying like prayer flags in the gentle Autumn breeze, each fluttering garment tethering her back to the world she loved.

As the buggy trundled forward, Esther's thoughts once more flickered unbidden to Eli. Their encounter at the harvest gathering had been charged—so full of unspoken words, regrets, and a simmering connection she could hardly acknowledge. She felt her heart flutter, and an unwelcome sense of apprehension settled deep within her, clouding the vibrant landscapes rolling by.

Stay focused, she told herself quietly, trying to extinguish the ache and the echo of longing she was desperate to deny. She could not afford the luxury of distraction now; Mammi Yoder needed her. And whatever awaited her at the Yoder farm—whatever tension lingered between her and Eli—would simply have to be endured.

As the buggy crested a hill, the sprawling Yoder farmhouse finally came into view, its wooden facade appearing rugged against the backdrop of the fading day. Nearby, Deborah's small cottage gleamed, sweet, white and unassuming. Seeing the place she knew Eli was, Esther tightened her grip on the herb basket, heart racing. The afternoon light gilded the moment, intertwining with her determination to be of service, just as her mother had taught her—rooted in faith, steeped in love.

As they stepped down from the wagon, the distant sound of an anxious crow echoed in the chill air. Deborah turned to Esther, her brow furrowed, her voice laced with concern. "I am so worried about *Mammi.* I know I am not a *doktor,* but between you and me, it does't look at all good."

The weight of those words settled on Esther, a reminder of the bond between her past and the present—her own knowledge becoming a lifeline not just for her, but perhaps for the Yoder family.

Esther nodded, steeling herself as they approached the door. She took a deep breath, the familiar scent of earth and weathered wood greeting her, and pushed it open.

Eli stood in the doorway to his grandmother's bedroom, tall and imposing. His frame appeared tense, as if the very act of standing had become an effort, the hollow darkness beneath his eyes revealing sleepless nights spent in worry.

His posture stiffened as he spotted Esther, arms folding across his chest defensively.

For a moment, their eyes locked, and in that instant, unspoken words hung heavy between them—the memory of his rejection at the harvest gathering, the betrothal to Martha hanging over them both like a storm cloud, and beneath it all, something neither of them dared name.

As if to punctuate the tension, a soft, labored sound came from the bedroom. It drew Esther's gaze past Eli— where Mammi Yoder lay, breathing shallow and strained, her normally vibrant face ashen against the white pillows. Anne Hostetler sat beside the bed, dabbing at the old woman's fevered brow with a damp cloth.

Esther's training immediately took over, pushing aside personal discomfort in the face of clear need. She stepped forward, her voice quiet but firm. "Eli, I'm here to help your mother. May I?"

For a heartbeat, he didn't move. She could see the conflict in his eyes—pride warring with desperation, his obvious need for help battling against whatever complicated feelings existed between them. His jaw worked, as if words were fighting to escape but couldn't find their way out.

Finally, he stepped aside, the movement jerky and reluctant. "She's been getting worse since yesterday," he said, his voice rough with exhaustion and worry. In the background, Anne discreetly rose, gathering her things before slipping away, her eyes flicking from Eli to Esther and back again. "Fever won't break… her breathing…" He trailed off, running a hand through his disheveled hair. Eli swallowed. *"Denki… go ahead."*

Esther moved past him into the dim bedroom, setting her basket down near the bedside with practiced care. The room smelled of sickness and worry, the air heavy and close. She approached Mammi Yoder with cautious optimism, her soft voice breaking the stillness.

"*Mammi*, it's Esther. Esther Troyer. I've come to help."

Her gaze drifted over the elderly woman's flushed face, noting the rapid pulse at her throat, the way her breath rattled in her chest. Esther reached out, brushing a few wisps of gray hair from Mammi's clammy forehead, her heart aching at the sight.

"Esther, *kinner*…" the old woman's voice was barely a whisper, crackling like dried leaves. "Is it really you?"

"It is, Mammi," Esther soothed, her own heart settling into the rhythm of care that came so naturally to her. "I'm going to make you more comfortable." She glanced back toward Eli, noting his silent vigilance from the doorway—a complex array of emotions playing across his handsome features.

Deborah, sensing the need for space amid the tension, offered Esther an encouraging nod before quietly excusing herself. "I'll check back tomorrow," she said softly, leaving Esther and Eli in the hushed atmosphere of the sickroom. "I'll be praying for her."

Left in the dim light, an uncomfortable stillness permeated the air, thick with the kind of worry that found no easy words. Esther looked back at Mammi Yoder, drawing upon her training, gathering thoughts and intentions like the very herbs she would soon use.

Eli remained poised in the doorway, watching as Esther began to assess what could be done.

"The fever needs to break," Esther said, more to herself than to him, but speaking aloud helped organize her thoughts. "And we need to ease her breathing." She began pulling herbs from her basket—elderberry for the fever, yarrow for its healing properties, mullein for the lungs.

"What do you need?" Eli's voice came from behind her,

startling her slightly. When she turned, she found he'd moved closer, his defensive posture softening into something more like helplessness. His grandmother's illness had stripped away the walls he'd erected between them.

"Hot water from the kettle," Esther replied, meeting his eyes directly for the first time since entering. "And help me lift her shoulders so she can drink."

He nodded, moving immediately to comply. As he gently raised his mother's frail form, his large hands surprisingly tender, Esther prepared the elderberry tea. The silence between them felt different now—less hostile, more like a truce born of necessity.

"Just a bit more, Mammi," Esther encouraged as she brought the cup to the old woman's lips, watching as the elderly woman's eyes flickered open, catching glimpses of recognition and trust. Eli held his grandmother steady, his face drawn with worry, and for a moment Esther forgot everything except the task before her.

When Mammi had drunk what she could, Eli carefully lowered her back to the pillows. He remained at the bedside, one hand resting on the wooden frame, his knuckles white with tension.

"Will she..." he started, then stopped, unable to finish the question.

"The next day or two will tell," Esther said honestly, already preparing a poultice. "But she's strong. And she's not alone." She met his eyes again, and something passed between them—an acknowledgment of shared purpose that transcended their personal complications.

As Esther worked, crushing yarrow and other herbs in a mortar and pestle she found in the kitchen, she felt Eli's presence hovering nearby. He watched her movements with an intensity that made her self-conscious, but she forced herself to focus on the task at hand.

"Your mother taught you all this?" he asked quietly, his voice carrying a note of something like admiration.

"*Ja*," Esther replied, her hands steady as she mixed the poultice. "She believed healing was a gift to be shared, not hoarded." She paused, then added softly, "I wish she were here now. She was far better at this than I am."

"I doubt that," Eli said, and when Esther glanced at him in surprise, she found him looking at her with an expression she couldn't quite read. "You have gentle hands. Skilled hands."

The compliment hung in the air between them, unexpected and tender. Esther felt warmth rise to her cheeks and quickly returned her attention to the poultice, trying to ignore the way her heart had suddenly started racing.

As the afternoon light filtered through the window, Esther applied the warm poultice to Mammi Yoder's chest, whispering a quiet prayer as she worked. With every touch, she sent small blessings into the herbal mixture—a whisper of hope wrapping around the family like a promise that healing could find its way even amid uncertainty.

When she finished and stepped back, she noticed Eli's shirt sleeve—a tear at the seam stood stark against the otherwise solid fabric, the uneven stitches a testament to his struggles. An unintentional reveal of his own vulnerabilities, and a reminder that he'd been managing alone, without a woman's care, for too long.

"Eli," Esther said softly, pointing to the torn sleeve. "Do you have a needle and thread?"

He looked down at his shirt as if seeing the tear for the first time, then back at her, uncertainty crossing his features. "You don't have to—"

"I know," Esther interrupted gently. "But I'm here, and it needs mending."

Without further argument, Eli produced a small sewing kit from a nearby drawer, laying it on the kitchen table. Their fingers brushed slightly as he handed it to her, the contact sending an unexpected spark through her that she quickly tried to ignore.

Esther settled by the fire where the light was best, and Eli stood awkwardly nearby in a fresh shirt he'd changed into, clearly unsure whether to stay or go. Finally, he lowered himself onto a chair across from her, watching as her needle moved through the fabric with small, perfect stitches.

"You make it look easy," he observed after a moment.

"Practice," Esther replied, a small smile tugging at her lips despite herself. "Lots and lots of practice. It's a *wunderbaar* thing when a stitch behaves My mother used to say that every stitch tells a story—whether you're patient or hurried, careful or careless."

"What story are these stitches telling?" Eli asked, and there was something in his voice that made her look up.

Their eyes met across the table, and Esther saw in his face a vulnerability she'd never witnessed before— exhaustion, yes, but also a loneliness that echoed her own. In that moment, the betrothal to Martha, the harvest gathering rejection—all of it seemed to fade, leaving only two people who had known each other all their lives and yet somehow not at all.

"They're telling a story of care," Esther said softly, returning to her stitching. "That's all." Even while saying it wondering why Martha had not done this small thing for her intended. Wasn't that what real love was about? The small things, the practical things as well as the romantic things? But perhaps Martha had her reasons.

When she finished, she folded the mended shirt carefully and set it on the table between them. "I should check on your grandmother before I go."

Mammi Yoder had fallen into a more peaceful sleep, her breathing still labored but less desperate. Esther adjusted the blankets and quilt and felt the old woman's forehead—still warm, but perhaps not quite as burning as before.

"I'll return tomorrow with more herbs," Esther promised, gathering her basket. "The fever should start to break by then if the tea and poultice work as they should."

She turned to leave, but Eli's voice stopped her at the door. "Esther."

She paused, looking back at him.

"Denki," he said simply, but the word carried a weight of sincerity that made her throat tighten. "For coming. For helping. For..." He gestured helplessly, unable to articulate everything he meant.

"Your mother would have done the same for mine," Esther replied softly. "That's what community means."

As she stepped out into the cool evening air, she heard him say, almost too quiet to catch, "It's more than that."

But when she turned back, he had already closed the door, and she was left standing in the gathering dusk, her heart full of questions she didn't dare ask aloud.

* * *

Esther's heart fluttered with anticipation as she stepped back onto the Yoder farm, the fresh basket of herbs cradled in her arm like a promise. The morning sun broke across the horizon, a gentle warmth washing over her as she approached the door, the weight of yesterday's connection lingering just beneath her skin like the memory of a half-forgotten dream.

Upon entering, the familiar scent of the farmhouse welcomed her—a blend of earthy undertones mixed with hints of lingering herbal fragrance from yesterday's remedies. As she stepped into the main room, she saw Mammi Yoder, sitting up in bed, her face still drawn but noticeably brighter, her eyes betraying an ember of strength flickering to life. Relief washed over Esther as she noted the small signs of improvement—subtle changes that rekindled hope deep within her heart.

"Mammi, it's *gut* to see you looking so much better today," Esther greeted, her voice soothing and filled with warmth.

She placed her basket on the worn wooden table and approached the bed, gently taking the elderly woman's hand into her own. The soft touch was reciprocated by a reassuring squeeze, and a small smile curled the corners of Mammi's lips, a flicker of gratitude lighting the room.

"Esther, dear," Mammi Yoder replied, her voice a mix of frailty and determination. "You're an angel sent from heaven itself, I think."

"Ach, nee, Mammi!" Though the elderly woman was not her own grandmother, everyone in Miracle Creek seemed to call her Mammi—and Esther was no exception. She was the kind of grandmother everyone wished they had, gentle, wise, and full of quiet, steadfast love.

With a chuckle, Esther straightened up, brushing her hair behind her ears as she assessed the remaining remedies in her basket. "Let's see what we can do to ensure that fever stays away for good, *ja?*"

As Esther retrieved the herbs—each with a story woven into their leaves and petals—she felt the rhythm of confidence return to her, flowing through her like a soft song. She began with the elderberry flowers, their soft, fragrant blooms a promise of resilience. Her hands moved with practiced grace, plucking, measuring, and crushing, each step reminiscent of lessons learned from her mother.

Eli appeared in the doorway, looking considerably better

than he had yesterday. He'd clearly managed a few hours of sleep, and the desperate edge had left his features, replaced by something softer—something like cautious hope. His eyes found Esther immediately, and she felt the weight of his gaze as she worked.

"How is she?" he asked, though he could see for himself the improvement.

"Better," Esther confirmed, mixing the elderberry flowers with hot water. "The fever has broken, though she's still weak. The next few days are critical—she needs rest, nourishment, and continued treatment. Make sure you contact the *doktor* or his wife the minute they are back."

Eli nodded, moving into the room with less hesitation than yesterday. "What can I do?"

As they worked together—Esther preparing remedies while Eli helped adjust pillows and fetch fresh water—a rhythm developed between them. The antagonism and awkwardness of yesterday had transformed into something else, a partnership born of shared purpose.

"Why use that herb?" Eli asked at one point, watching as Esther carefully measured out chamomile.

"Chamomile soothes and helps with sleep," Esther explained, appreciating his genuine interest. "Rest is as important as any medicine. The body heals itself when given the chance—we just help it along."

"Your mother taught you well," Eli observed, and Esther caught the note of respect in his voice that made her cheeks warm.

"She believed healing was a calling," Esther replied softly. "A way to serve *Gott* by serving His people."

As Mammi Yoder sipped the chamomile tea, her eyes moved between Esther and her grandson, a knowing look passing over her weathered features. "You two make a *gut* team," she said, her voice still weak but touched with something that sounded almost like satisfaction.

Both Esther and Eli shifted uncomfortably, suddenly hyperaware of how naturally they'd been working together. Esther busied herself organizing the remaining herbs while Eli found sudden fascination with adjusting the window curtains.

"Now then," Mammi continued, settling back against her pillows with a contented sigh, "don't let an old woman embarrass you. I'm just grateful for the help." But her eyes sparkled with a wisdom that suggested she saw far more than they realized.

After ensuring Mammi was comfortable, Esther prepared to leave, but Eli followed her to the door.

"Will you... will you come back tomorrow?" he asked, and there was something vulnerable in the question that made Esther's heart skip.

"Of course," she replied. "Until she's fully recovered."

"Denki, Esther," he murmured. "And after?" The words slipped out before Eli seemed to realize he'd said them, and he looked almost startled by his own boldness.

Esther paused, her hand on the door frame, acutely aware of all the reasons she should walk away—Martha, the betrothal, the community's expectations, her own wounded heart. But when she looked at Eli, she saw the same conflict she felt, the same war between duty and desire.

"We'll see," she said softly, and left before either of them could say anything more.

* * *

By the third day, Mammi Yoder's improvement was undeniable. She sat fully upright in bed, color restored to her cheeks, even managing to tease Esther about her careful measurements of herbs.

"You fuss over those plants like a mother hen," Mammi chuckled, her voice stronger now. "Half a pinch more won't hurt anything."

"Precision matters," Esther protested with a smile, but she was delighted to see the old woman's spirit returning.

Eli had been working in the fields that morning, and when he came in for the midday meal, Esther was startled by the transformation in him. The desperate worry that had lined his face was gone, replaced by something lighter. When he saw his grandmother sitting up, laughing at something Esther had said, his entire face illuminated with relief and joy.

"She's herself again," he said to Esther, wonder in his voice.

"She's strong," Esther replied. "The pneumonia is passing. Another few days of rest and she'll be back to scolding you about muddy boots."

"I heard that," Mammi called from the bedroom, making them both laugh.

As Esther prepared to leave, Eli walked her outside. The autumn afternoon was crisp and golden, leaves swirling in lazy spirals around the farmyard.

"I can't thank you enough," Eli said, stopping near her buggy. "You saved her life. The *doktor* wouldn't have returned in time, and I…" His voice caught. "I didn't know what to do."

"You did exactly right by sending for help," Esther assured him. "And by being here for her. That matters far more than any herb I brought."

They stood in the golden light, and Esther knew she should leave, should climb into her buggy and put distance between herself and this complicated, impossible situation. But Eli was looking at her with such gratitude, such warmth, that her feet seemed rooted to the ground.

"Esther, I—" he started, then stopped, his jaw working as if trying to find words that wouldn't come.

The moment stretched between them, heavy with possibility. Esther's heart hammered in her chest, hoping and fearing in equal measure what he might say.

But then the sound of an approaching buggy broke the spell. They both turned to see Martha Stoltzfus arriving, her father at the reins. Martha's eyes immediately found Eli, then moved to Esther, and something cool and assessing entered her expression.

"I heard your grandmother was ill, Eli," Martha said, three days late, as she climbed down, her voice pleasant but her eyes sharp. "I've brought soup and bread."

"That's kind of you," Eli replied, but his voice had gone flat, the warmth of moments before evaporating.

Esther gathered her basket quickly. "I should be going. Mammi is much improved—she won't need me tomorrow."

"Wait!" Eli said, but Esther was already climbing into her buggy, unable to bear the weight of Martha's measuring gaze, unable to watch Eli shift into his role as dutiful intended husband.

As she drove away, she glanced back once to see Eli still standing in the yard, watching her leave while Martha waited at his side. The image burned itself into Esther's memory—a perfect picture of the impossible divide between them.

That night, as Esther lay in bed, she pressed Eli's mended shirt to her chest, inhaling his mannish scent— he'd insisted she take it to repair one more small tear she'd noticed. In the darkness, she allowed herself to acknowledge the truth: she was falling even deeper in love with a man promised to someone else, and every moment she spent near him only tangled her heart more hopelessly.

She whispered a prayer into the darkness: "Lord, give me strength to do what's right, even when my heart is breaking. And if this door is closed, help me to walk away."

But even as she prayed for strength to leave, a small, stubborn part of her heart whispered that perhaps—just perhaps—some doors weren't meant to stay closed forever. That some Red Seas do part.

Chapter 4
Seeds of Friendship

Esther stepped into the golden morning light, the promise of warmth radiating through the cool air as she made her way toward the Yoder farmhouse. The path was familiar now, worn smooth by her visits over the past week. The tall grasses swayed gently like a welcoming embrace as she neared the front door, her basket filled with herbs for what she told herself would be her final visit—Mammi Yoder was nearly recovered, after all.

Each step echoed her conflicted purpose—a mixture of duty to ensure the elderly woman's full recovery and an unspoken longing she could no longer deny. She hoped her efforts would bring complete healing to Mammi Yoder, yet beneath the surface lurked the knowledge that once her patient was well, she would have no reason to return. No reason to see Eli.

As she approached, she admired the sturdy wooden structure, its worn planks absorbing the sunlight that streamed through the trees. The space was a comforting sight, yet something stirred unease in her heart—the weight of Martha's claim on this place, on this family, on Eli himself.

Entering the farmhouse, she was immediately greeted by the earthy scent of home—milled wood, herbs, and the remnants of breakfast. The warmth of the sun pouring through the window wrapped her in an embrace of familiarity.

Esther moved through the main room, where worn furniture told stories of many seasons spent in laughter and love. Her heart fluttered with a quiet anticipation as she stepped into Mammi Yoder's room, where a thin beam of light illuminated the old woman sitting fully upright in bed, color restored to her weathered cheeks.

"Mammi, you're looking *gut*—truly *wunderbaar*," Esther said, genuine delight warming her voice as she approached. The transformation was remarkable—just days ago, this vibrant woman had been barely clinging to life.

"Thanks to you, dear child," Mammi replied, her voice strong and clear. She patted the edge of the bed. "Come, sit with me a moment. We should talk."

Esther settled beside her, unpacking a few final herbs from her basket. "I've brought elderberry tea for you to continue taking, just for another few days to build your strength."

"Always so careful, so thorough," Mammi observed, her keen eyes studying Esther's face. ""*Ach, Kinner,* just like your *Mamm*. She had healing hands too, you know. And a *gut* heart." The old woman paused, then added meaningfully, "She also knew when to speak up for what she wanted, and when she stayed silent too long, she regretted it."

Esther's hands stilled over the herbs, understanding the layered meaning in Mammi's words. Before she could respond, voices drifted from the kitchen—Eli speaking with someone, the tone practical and measured.

"The harvest is *gut* this year, but the debts remain," Eli was saying.

Esther's stomach sank as she recognized the second voice—Martha's father, no doubt discussing the financial arrangements that would bound the two families together, the joining of land as well of hands. The betrothal wasn't just about land and tradition; it was about survival, about Eli's ability to keep his farm and care for his grandmother.

Mammi Yoder sighed softly, and when Esther met her eyes, she saw sadness there. "Some chains are forged by necessity rather than desire," the old woman said quietly. "My grandson believes he has no choice. Sometimes the young are so busy being practical that they forget about joy."

Esther's throat tightened. "He's doing what's right for his family."

"Is he?" Mammi challenged gently. "Or is he doing what's expected? There's a difference, child." She reached out and took Esther's hand in her frail but determined grip. "I've seen how he looks at you when he thinks no one's watching. And I've seen how you look at him."

"Mammi, I—" Esther's protest died on her lips as the old woman squeezed her hand.

"I won't live forever, Esther. And when I'm gone, I want to know my grandson has chosen happiness, not just duty. Promise me you'll think about that."

Before Esther could respond, Eli appeared in the doorway, his expression brightening when he saw his grandmother sitting up so vigorously. "You're looking well, Mammi."

"Thanks to our Esther here," Mammi said, releasing Esther's hand but holding her gaze for one meaningful moment longer.

The voices from the kitchen had faded—Martha's father had apparently left. Esther stood, smoothing her apron with nervous hands. "I should check the kitchen. You mentioned the dishes had piled up?"

It was true—in the chaos of Mammi's illness, household tasks had fallen by the wayside. The kitchen bore evidence of a household without a woman's regular care, and Esther found herself unable to simply walk away from the disorder.

Though she lived only on the neighboring farm, Martha showed little interest in providing Eli with any practical help. Sewing, cooking, the daily tasks essential to keeping the household running—none of it seemed to concern her. Forget doing it for the one you loved; what about simply being a *gut* neighbor?

"You don't have to—" Eli started, but Esther was already rolling up her sleeves.

"I'm here anyway," she said, more briskly than she felt. "It won't take long."

What she didn't say was that she needed something to do with her hands, some task to occupy her mind and prevent it from dwelling on Mammi's words or the impossible situation she found herself in.

* * *

The kitchen pulsed with quiet activity as Esther and Eli worked side by side, the morning sun streaming through the window and illuminating the space with golden light. Dust motes danced in the air between them, and the simple domesticity of the moment—washing dishes, organizing supplies—felt simultaneously natural and dangerous.

Esther stood at the washbasin, her hands submerged in warm, soapy water, methodically cleaning the accumulated dishes. Eli stood beside her with a cloth, drying each plate and cup she passed to him. Their movements developed a rhythm, a silent choreography that spoke of an ease that shouldn't exist between them.

"You don't have to help," Esther said softly, acutely aware of how close he stood, how their shoulders occasionally brushed as they worked.

"It's my kitchen," Eli replied with a slight smile. "Seems only right I should know where things go."

A comfortable silence settled between them, broken only by the gentle splash of water and the clink of dishes.

Esther found herself stealing glances at him—the strong line of his jaw, the way his rolled-up sleeves revealed forearms bronzed by farmwork, the small scar near his temple that she'd never noticed before.

"I remember you from school," Eli said suddenly, his voice quiet but clear. "Do you remember the day I forgot my lunch?"

Esther's hands stilled in the water. *"Ja.* I remember."

"You shared yours with me without hesitation. Half your sandwich, your apple, even the cookies your mother had packed." He paused in his drying, the cloth hanging loosely in his hands, his eye's distant. "They were delicious! As *gut* as Emma Albrecht's…. But I was so embarrassed. New to the school, didn't know anyone, and I'd been so nervous that morning I'd run out the door without my pail."

"You were… what? Eight years old?" Esther said softly, resuming her washing to hide the trembling in her hands. "It seemed the natural thing to do."

"It wasn't just that you shared," Eli continued, and she could hear something deeper in his voice now. "It was the way you did it. Like it was nothing special, like you couldn't imagine doing anything else. You sat with me that whole lunch period, told me about the other scholars, made me feel less alone." He set down the plate he'd been drying and turned to face her more fully. "I never forgot that kindness, Esther. It's stayed with me all these years."

Esther's breath caught in her throat. She pulled her hands from the water, reaching for a cloth to dry them, needing something to do to steady herself. "It was just lunch, Eli."

"No," he said firmly. "It was more than that. It was you seeing someone who needed help and helping them. The way you helped my grandmother last week. The way you

—" He stopped abruptly, seeming to catch himself, but his eyes remained on her face with an intensity that made her knees weak.

"The way I what?" Esther whispered, unable to stop herself from asking.

Eli opened his mouth, then closed it again. She watched conflict play across his features—duty warring with desire, obligation battling against longing. Finally, he said, "The way you care for people. It's a gift."

It wasn't what he'd been about to say, and they both knew it. The unspoken words hung between them like morning mist, visible but intangible.

Esther turned back to the basin, desperate to break the spell of the moment before she said something she couldn't take back. Her hands plunged into the cooling water, grasping for the next dish, but Eli's hand was already there, reaching for the same plate.

Their fingers met beneath the surface, warm skin against warm skin. Neither of them pulled away immediately. The touch lasted only seconds but felt like an eternity—an acknowledgment of everything they couldn't say, everything that stood between them.

When they finally drew back, both of them moved with jerky, self-conscious motions. Esther scrubbed at a plate that was already clean, while Eli dried a cup with unnecessary vigor.

"I should make something for your midday meal," Esther said, her voice higher than normal. "You'll need proper food to keep your strength up for the field work."

"Esther, you don't need to—"

"I want to," she interrupted, meeting his eyes with a directness that surprised them both. "Let me do this. Please."

There was a wealth of meaning in her request that had

nothing to do with cooking. Let me care for you. Let me be here. Let me pretend, just for a little while, that this could be my life."

Eli nodded slowly, understanding more than she'd said. "I'd like that."

They worked together preparing a simple meal—bread, cold meat, preserves, nothing elaborate but done with care. As Esther sliced the bread, Eli moved around the kitchen gathering plates and utensils, their movements developing that same easy synchronization that felt both right and terribly wrong.

"Tell me about your quilting," Eli said as they worked. "I've heard people say your patterns are beautiful. Where do you find the designs?"

Esther looked up, surprised by his interest. "Some are traditional patterns my mother taught me. Others... I see them in the world around me. The way frost forms on a window. The pattern of fields at harvest time. The way light falls through leaves."

"You see beauty everywhere," Eli observed, and there was something almost wistful in his tone.

"Don't you?" Esther asked. "Your cornfields in the morning mist, the way your barn swallows make their nests, even the pattern of furrows after plowing—there's beauty in all of it if you look."

"I suppose I've been too busy working to notice," Eli admitted. "But you make me want to look closer. To see what you see."

The words hung between them, laden with meaning neither could fully acknowledge. They were talking about more than quilting patterns and farmland beauty—they were talking about perspective, about the different ways they moved through the world, about the connection that seemed to exist between their very ways of seeing.

Esther set the sliced bread on a plate, her hands trembling slightly. "Eli, I should tell you—"

But whatever she'd been about to say was interrupted by the sound of a wagon approaching outside. They both turned toward the window, and Esther's heart sank as she recognized the vehicle.

Martha Stoltzfus, and this time she wasn't alone. Several women from the community accompanied her, including Sarah Mathews, the *doktor's* wife, newly back from Tall Poplars, and Veronica Zook, no doubt coming to check on Mammi Yoder's recovery and the latter—Esther suspected —to assess the situation between Eli and his intended bride.

"I should go," Esther said quickly, already untying her apron.

"Wait," Eli said, his hand reaching out as if to stop her, but falling short of actual contact. "Esther, please—"

"You have visitors," Esther said, forcing brightness into her voice even as her heart cracked. "And your mother is well enough now that she doesn't need me anymore. This was always meant to be temporary."

She gathered her basket with quick, efficient movements, avoiding his gaze because she knew if she looked at him now, she might not be able to leave. As she moved toward the door, she heard Martha's voice outside, bright and proprietorial, calling out greetings.

"*Denki,*" Eli said softly behind her. "For everything."

Esther paused at the door, her back to him, one hand on the frame. Without turning around, she whispered, "Take care of yourself, Eli Yoder."

Then she slipped out the back door, avoiding the group at the front, and made her way to where her buggy waited. As she drove away, she didn't look back—couldn't look back—because she knew what she'd see: Eli standing in the doorway of his home, Martha at his side where Esther could never be, the future stretching out before them on a path that had no room for what might have been.

But she couldn't stop the tears that came, silent and insistent, as the Yoder farm disappeared behind her and the weight of reality settled once more upon her shoulders. She'd gone there to heal Mammi Yoder, and she'd succeeded with *Gott's* help. What she hadn't anticipated was how much the visits would wound her own heart—or how difficult it would be to walk away from the one place that had started to feel like home.

* * *

That evening, Esther sat at her own family's table for supper, pushing food around her plate while Mae chattered about the day's events and their father read quietly from his Bible. Her mother's empty chair seemed more pronounced than usual, a reminder of loss and all the conversations she could never have, all the advice she'd never receive.

"Esther, you've barely eaten," Daniel observed, setting down his Bible. "Are you feeling well?"

"Just tired, *Datt*," Esther replied, managing a small smile. "It's been a full week what with caring for Mammi Yoder."

"The community is grateful for your help," Daniel said, his eyes kind but searching. "Eli Yoder spoke to me at the construction site I was working at today. He said his mother's recovery is entirely due to your skill with herbs."

Esther's heart skipped. "He's too generous. Mammi Yoder is strong. She would have recovered."

"Perhaps," Daniel said thoughtfully. "But strength alone doesn't always suffice. Sometimes we need help—and the wisdom to accept it when it's offered."

There was something in his tone that made Esther look up sharply, but her father had already returned to his reading, his expression placid. Had Eli said something else? Had Daniel noticed something in the way Eli spoke of her?

"Martha Stoltzfus told me she's planning to start learning to manage the Yoder household," Mae piped up, seemingly oblivious to the way Esther's hands tightened on her fork. "She says after the wedding, she'll be making changes to the kitchen arrangement."

Esther felt each word like a small blade. Martha, planning her life in Eli's home. Martha, who would stand at that kitchen window and watch the seasons change. Martha, who would sleep beside Eli and bear his children and grow old in the home that Esther had, for one brief week, allowed herself to imagine might somehow become hers.

And yet this was the same Martha who had shown so little apparent concern for the household in the present. Though she was not 'obliged' to as she was not Eli's wife yet, it was nonetheless the *right* thing and it was so unAmish not to. Perhaps Martha liked to talk more than act. Esther's mind went to Philippians: *God causes us both to will and to act according to His good purpose.* She remembered Bishop Samuel Lapp's words explaining the verse. He said it was about not merely 'willing' to do something, but following it through in actions—*doing*. And surely *Gott's gut* purpose included caring for neighbors.

"Martha has ideas about how things should be organized." Mae continued. "She said she will make it real pretty."

"That's as it should be," Daniel said mildly, his expression inscrutable. "A *fraa* should have authority in her own household."

But she doesn't love him, Esther wanted to scream. *Not the way I do. She sees him as a duty, a practical arrangement, a trophy not as...*

Not as what? Not as the man whose rare smile made her heart sing? Not as the boy who had never forgotten a shared lunch? Not as someone whose very presence made the world feel more vivid and alive?

"May I be excused?" Esther asked, her voice strained.

Daniel studied her for a long moment, then nodded. "Go on, *dochder.* Rest."

Esther fled to her room, where she lit a single candle and sat at her small desk. Her journal lay before her—the one place she allowed herself complete honesty. She opened it to a fresh page and began to write, her hand moving almost without conscious thought:

His eyes hold summer fields,
His hands speak gentleness and strength,
His smile—so rare—could melt
The winter from my heart.

Now another holds
The place I dared not claim,
And I must watch him wed
And bear another's name.

Lord, grant me strength to smile,
To wish them joy and peace,
To hide this breaking heart
And pray for love's release.

She set down her pen and stared at the words—the most honest thing she'd ever written about her feelings for Eli. Then, with trembling hands, she carefully tore the page from her journal, folded it, and tucked it between the pages near the back of the book.

Some truths were too dangerous to leave easily visible. Some confessions could never be spoken aloud. But at least here, in ink on paper, her heart had finally found its voice —even if it was a voice that would never be heard.

Chapter 5
Stormy Hearts

The sun hung high over the Lancaster fields, gilding the scene with a warm glow that suffused the bustling Graber farm. Laughter and lively chatter danced through the air, twining together in the vibrant hum of community as Esther stood at the edge of a gathering for the much-anticipated barn-raising. Platters of golden bread and sliced meats lay arrayed before her, a fragrant feast prepared with care.

The barn-raising was a sight to behold, with men working together in focused camaraderie, their strong arms lifting beams as they constructed a sturdy shelter that would soon echo with the laughter of shared moments. The rhythmic sound of hammers striking nails merged with the excited shouts of children darting between the adults, their laughter as sweet as the aroma of freshly baked goods wafting on the gentle breeze.

Esther felt the warmth of the day envelop her as she moved among the tables, arranging the platters with practiced ease born from countless gatherings just like this one.

Around her, women clustered in small groups, their capable hands preparing food while their voices wove together in comfortable conversation. Esther worked alongside them, slicing bread and arranging pickles, but her attention kept drifting toward the construction site where the men labored.

"Esther, dear, could you bring those pastries over here?" Dorcas Hershberger called, her hands busy arranging serving dishes.

Esther nodded, gathering the delicate treats she had

spent the previous evening crafting. As she moved to comply, her gaze caught on a familiar figure among the workers—Eli Yoder, his shirt clinging to his broad shoulders as he maneuvered a heavy beam into place alongside three other men.

She couldn't help but watch as he worked, the late morning sun catching the sheen of perspiration on his brow. When he paused to wipe his face with his forearm, pushing the fabric of his sleeve across his forehead, something in Esther's chest tightened with a longing she could no longer deny.

"Quite a sight, isn't it?" Mae appeared at her elbow, her voice low and knowing. "The way a man works with his hands, building something that will stand for generations."

"Mae," Esther warned softly, but her sister only smiled.

"I'm just saying what every woman here is thinking. Though most of them have a right to look." The implication was clear—Esther didn't, not with Martha's claim on Eli becoming more solid by the day.

As if summoned by the thought, Martha appeared among the women's group, carrying a large basket. She moved with confidence, greeting the older women, especially Dorcas and Veronica, with easy familiarity, already acting the part of Eli's wife though no formal announcement had been made.

"I've brought apple tarts," Martha announced brightly. "Eli's favorite. I've been practicing the recipe his grandmother taught me."

Several women made approving sounds, and Esther felt her stomach twist. Of course Martha had been learning Mammi Yoder's recipes. Of course she was already being welcomed into the intimate knowledge of Eli's preferences and family traditions. This was how it should be, how it would be.

"They look wonderful," Esther managed to say, her voice steady despite the ache in her chest.

Martha's gaze slid to her, assessing and cool. "Thank you, Esther. I heard you did wonderful work caring for Mammi Yoder during her illness. The family is very grateful." The words were polite, but there was an edge beneath them—a subtle claiming of territory, a reminder that Martha spoke for "the family" now. Even though her absence and lack of practical care had been noted during the crisis.

"I was glad to help," Esther replied simply, returning to her work with deliberate focus.

The morning wore on, the barn structure rising board by board, the community working in the synchronized rhythm of long practice. Esther found herself tasked with bringing fresh water to the workers, and she couldn't avoid the moment she'd been both dreading and anticipating.

She approached the work site with a pitcher and cups, her heart hammering in her chest. Several men gratefully accepted the water, offering thanks between gulps. And then she was standing before Eli, a cup extended toward him, acutely aware of the watching eyes around them.

Eli's eyes met hers, and for a heartbeat the world seemed to narrow to just the two of them. She saw recognition there, and something deeper—a yearning that mirrored her own. His hand reached toward the cup she offered, and for a suspended moment their fingers nearly touched.

Then, as if catching himself, Eli's expression shuttered. He pulled his hand back, his jaw tightening. "Thank you, but I'm fine," he said gruffly, his voice carrying none of the warmth that had been in his eyes just seconds before.

The rejection stung like a physical blow, especially as it echoed his previous rejection at the harvest gathering.

Esther felt heat rise to her cheeks as awareness of the watching eyes around them prickled along her skin. She nodded once, unable to trust her voice, and moved on to the next worker.

What she couldn't know—what Eli couldn't tell her—was that the rejection had nothing to do with want and everything to do with self-preservation. Seeing her there, her gentle smile offering kindness, had nearly broken his resolve entirely. He'd almost reached for her hand along with the cup, almost pulled her aside to tell her everything.

But Martha was as always when community was around somewhere nearby. He couldn't accept Esther's kindness when every interaction with her made him question the path he'd chosen, made him wonder if he'd made the biggest mistake of his life.

From across the work site, Martha had witnessed the exchange. Her eyes narrowed slightly as she watched Esther move away, noting the flush on the younger woman's cheeks, the way Eli stood rigid and tense even as he returned to his work with unusual vigor.

"Bishop Lapp," Martha said, approaching the bishop where he stood supervising the construction. "Might I have a word?"

As the afternoon progressed, Esther found herself increasingly isolated. Women who had been friendly earlier now seemed distant, their conversations falling silent when she approached. She told herself she was imagining it, that her own guilt and confusion were making her paranoid.

But when Bishop Samuel Lapp approached her father, speaking in low tones while glancing in her direction, Esther knew something had shifted. The barn-raising continued around her, but she felt suddenly apart from it all, as if she stood behind glass watching life happen without her.

"Esther," her father said quietly, appearing at her side. "I need you to fetch more supplies from the storage barn. Take your sister with you."

It was a simple request, innocuous on its surface. But Esther caught the meaningful look in her father's eyes—he was removing her from a situation that was becoming complicated, giving her a reason to be away from Eli's presence, from Martha's watchful gaze, from the knowing looks of the community.

"Yes, *Datt*," she said softly.

As she and Mae made their way toward the old storage barn at the edge of the Graber property, dark clouds began gathering on the horizon. The air grew heavy and thick, carrying the promise of rain.

"They're talking about you," Mae said bluntly once they were out of earshot. "Martha spoke to the bishop. Said she's concerned about the amount of time you spent at the Yoder farm, that it wasn't proper for an unmarried woman to be alone so often with her intended."

Esther's steps faltered. "I was caring for his grandmother. Deborah called for me! There was nothing improper—"

"I know that, and you know that," Mae interrupted. "But Martha is making sure everyone understands her claim. She's being very clever about it—all concern and propriety, no direct accusations. But the message is clear. I overheard them, you know."

Esther felt sick. Her acts of charity, her genuine care for Mammi Yoder, were being twisted into something sordid. Normally she would have told her *schwester* off for eavesdropping, but instead she saught more information. "What did the bishop say?"

"That he trusts in your virtue and character," Mae replied. "But also that it would be wise to be mindful of appearances going forward. *Datt* isn't angry, Esther, but he's worried. He can see what's happening."

"What's happening?" Esther asked, though she knew the answer.

"You're in love with Eli Yoder," Mae said simply. "And he's in love with you. And neither of you will admit it, and now it's too late, and it's breaking both of your hearts."

Esther stopped walking entirely, turning to face her sister in shock. "Mae—"

"Don't deny it," Mae said firmly, her young face unusually serious. "I've been watching you both for weeks. The way he looks at you when he thinks no one's watching. The way you look at him all the time. It's written all over both of you."

Thunder rumbled in the distance, and the first fat drops of rain began to fall.

"It doesn't matter," Esther said, her voice breaking. "He's betrothed to Martha. Whatever I feel or don't feel is irrelevant."

"But what if—"

"There is no 'what if," Esther said firmly, blinking back tears that she told herself were just from the wind. "Come on, we need to get those supplies."

They hurried toward the storage barn, but the rain came faster than expected. By the time they reached the old structure, the sky had opened up, rain drumming against the roof in a deafening rhythm. They pushed through the door, laughing breathlessly at their narrow escape from a complete soaking.

The barn was dim and musty, lit only by the gray light filtering through small windows. Stacks of supplies lined the walls—nails, tools, extra lumber, all organized for easy access during the building. Esther and Mae began gathering what they needed, working efficiently despite the gloom.

"This rain won't last long," Mae observed, peering out at the downpour. "October storms never do."

But even as she spoke, lightning flashed, followed immediately by a crack of thunder that shook the barn walls. The rain intensified, and through the window they could see people running for shelter, the barn-raising temporarily abandoned.

"Or maybe it will," Mae amended.

Esther was reaching for a box of nails when she heard the barn door creak open behind them. She turned, expecting to see another worker seeking shelter from the storm.

Instead, Eli Yoder stood in the doorway, rain-soaked and breathing hard as if he'd run the whole way. His eyes found Esther immediately, and the intensity in them made her breath catch.

"Eli," she said, barely a whisper.

"I saw you come this way," he said, his voice rough. "The floor's flooding in here—water's coming through the wall cracks. You need to get to higher ground."

As if to emphasize his words, Esther looked down to see water indeed beginning to seep across the barn floor, pooling in the low spots. The rain was coming so hard and fast that the old barn couldn't keep it out.

"There's a loft," Eli said, pointing to a ladder that led to a hay storage area above. "Up there, quickly."

"I'll go first," Mae said, already moving toward the ladder. But as she grabbed the first rung, her foot slipped on the wet floor. She caught herself, but looked up at the ladder with new wariness. "These rungs are slick with water."

"Carefully then," Eli said, moving to steady the ladder. "I'll hold it for you."

Mae climbed slowly, testing each rung. When she reached the top, she looked down at Esther and Eli, and something shifted in her expression—a calculation, a decision.

"Esther, there's some old blankets up here," Mae called down. "But they're at the far end, past all these hay bales. I'm going to have to move some of them to get to the dry ones. This might take a few minutes."

It was a transparent excuse, and all three of them knew it. Mae was giving Esther and Eli time alone, creating a situation where propriety demanded they shelter together while she played chaperone from a distance.

Esther opened her mouth to protest, but another crash of thunder drowned out her words. Eli gestured to the ladder.

"Go on," he said. "I'll follow."

With her heart in her throat, Esther climbed the ladder, acutely aware of Eli below her, steadying her ascent. When she reached the top, she pulled herself into the loft, and moments later Eli joined her.

The loft was a confined space, barely six feet high at its peak, filled with hay bales stacked haphazardly. The rain drummed against the roof above them, and through a small window they could see the storm raging outside. True to her word, Mae had disappeared behind a wall of hay bales at the far end, giving them the illusion of privacy.

Esther found a relatively stable hay bale and sat, trying to calm her racing heart. Eli remained standing for a moment, then slowly lowered himself onto a bale across from her, close enough that their knees nearly touched in the cramped space.

For a long moment, they simply sat in the dim, dusty light, the storm raging around them, the weight of everything unsaid pressing down like the heavy air before lightning strikes.

"Esther," Eli finally said, his voice low and urgent. "I need to explain—"

"You don't owe me any explanations," Esther interrupted, unable to bear hearing him talk about duty or Martha or all the reasons why what existed between them could never be.

"But I do," Eli insisted. "When I refused the water—"

"You were right to," Esther said quickly. "It was improper of me to put you in that position, with Martha there, with everyone watching—"

"That's not why I refused." The words came out harsh, almost angry, and Esther looked up at him in surprise. His hands were clenched on his knees, his jaw tight. "I refused because I wanted to accept it too much. Because every time you're near me, I forget every sensible reason why I shouldn't…"

He trailed off, but the unfinished sentence hung between them, electric with meaning.

"Why you shouldn't what?" Esther whispered, even though she knew she shouldn't ask, shouldn't push, shouldn't let this conversation continue.

Eli's eyes met hers, and in the flash of lightning that illuminated the loft, she saw his resolve crumbling. "Why I shouldn't tell you the truth."

Thunder crashed around them, and in that moment, something broke loose—all the restraint, all the propriety, all the careful distance they'd tried to maintain.

"What truth?" Esther asked, her voice barely audible over the storm.

"That five years ago, I came to your house," Eli said, the words tumbling out now as if he couldn't hold them back any longer. "I was going to ask your father's permission to court you. I'd been working up the courage for weeks. It was just past your seventeenth birthday. I remember, I picked wildflowers like a fool, rehearsed what I'd say—"

Esther's breath caught. "What?"

"But then I heard you," Eli continued, his voice raw with old pain. "Through the kitchen window. Your sister was teasing you, asking if you were sweet on me. And you said…" He stopped, swallowing hard. "You said you had no interest in me that way. None at all. You sounded so certain, so embarrassed by the very suggestion."

Esther felt the blood drain from her face as memory crashed over her. That day. That terrible day when Mae had been teasing her mercilessly, when she'd been terrified someone might overhear and spread gossip, when she'd denied her feelings out of pure mortification.

"Eli," she breathed, horror and understanding flooding through her. "You were there? You heard that?"

"Every word," he said quietly. "I stood there with those ridiculous flowers wilting in my hands, feeling like the biggest fool in Lancaster County. So I left. And then when Martha started showing interest, when our fathers started talking about a practical arrangement between families…" He shrugged helplessly. "I told myself it was for the best. That I'd been saved from humiliating myself."

"Oh, Eli," Esther whispered, tears streaming down her face now. "I didn't mean it. I was embarrassed—Mae had been teasing me all day, and I was afraid someone would overhear and gossip, and I just—I said what I thought I should say, not what was true."

His head snapped up, eyes searching her face. "What?"

"I've cared for you for ten years," Esther confessed, the words she'd never dared speak finally breaking free. "I've watched you and hoped and prayed and been too afraid to ever say anything because I thought—I thought you could never see me that way."

They stared at each other in the flickering light, the magnitude of their misunderstanding hanging between them like a physical thing. All this pain, all this heartache, born from a moment of cowardice and an overheard lie.

"Esther," Eli said hoarsely, and then he was moving, closing the small distance between them, reaching for her hands. "All this time?"

"All this time," she confirmed, looking down at their joined hands, his rough and calloused, hers still soft despite the work she did. "But it doesn't change anything, does it? You're still betrothed to Martha."

"I don't love her," Eli said urgently. "I respect her, I'll honor my commitment to her, but I don't—I can't—" He broke off, frustrated. "How can I marry her when my heart belongs to someone else?"

Esther's breath hitched at the admission, but even as joy flared in her chest, reality crashed back down. "You have to. Breaking the betrothal would shame both families, hurt Martha, possibly cost you the farm."

"I know," Eli said, anguish clear in his voice. "I know all of that. But Esther—"

Whatever he'd been about to say was cut off by Mae's voice calling from the other end of the loft. "The rain is letting up! We should get back before people worry!"

Reality intruded like cold water. Esther pulled her hands from Eli's, the loss of contact almost painful. They couldn't be found like this—sitting close, hands clasped, tears on both their faces. The scandal would destroy them both.

"She's right," Esther said, wiping her eyes quickly. "We should go."

"Esther, wait—we can't just leave it like this—"

"What else can we do?" Esther asked, her voice breaking. "You're promised to another. I can't—we can't —" She stood abruptly, nearly hitting her head on the low roof. "This was a mistake. We should never have—"

"Don't," Eli said fiercely, standing as well. "Don't call this a mistake. Finally knowing the truth—that's not a mistake."

"But what *gut* does the truth do us now?" Esther asked, fresh tears spilling over. "It only makes everything hurt more. For me at least!"

She moved toward the ladder, desperate to escape before she broke down completely. But as she reached for the first rung, Eli caught her arm gently.

"I don't know what to do," he admitted quietly. "But I had to tell you. You deserved to know that you weren't wrong—what you felt, what I felt, it was real. It is real."

Esther looked back at him, memorizing his face in the dim light—the way his wet hair curled slightly at his temple, the desperate honesty in his eyes, the set of his jaw that spoke of determination even in the face of impossible odds.

"I know," she whispered. "But real doesn't always mean possible."

Then she descended the ladder quickly, before her resolve could crumble entirely. Mae appeared, shooting Eli a complex look—part apology, part understanding, part warning—before following her sister down.

By the time Eli emerged from the barn, the rain had indeed slowed to a drizzle. People were beginning to emerge from their shelters, preparing to resume work. And there, near the main construction site, stood Martha with Esther's father and the bishop, her expression carefully neutral but her eyes sharp as they tracked Eli's appearance from the storage barn.

Esther hurried back to the food tables, keeping her head down, trying to compose herself. But she could feel the weight of watching eyes, could sense the subtle shift in the air around her. Whatever Martha had said to the bishop earlier had planted seeds of suspicion, and her extended absence with Eli—even chaperoned by Mae—would only water them.

As the day wore on and the barn-raising resumed, Esther worked mechanically, responding when spoken to but feeling as if she moved through a dream. Across the yard, Eli returned to his labor with grim determination, attacking the work as if he could somehow hammer away his confusion and heartache.

And between them, unspoken but undeniable, lay the truth they'd finally shared—a truth that changed everything and nothing, that illuminated their past even as it shadowed their future, that would haunt them both in the long, lonely days ahead.

As the sun began to sink toward the horizon, casting long shadows across the newly raised barn frame, Esther gathered her things to leave. She allowed herself one last glance toward where Eli worked, and found him already looking at her. Their eyes met across the distance, and in that moment, no words were needed.

They both knew what they stood to lose. They both knew what duty demanded. And they both knew that sometimes, love wasn't enough—not when weighed against family, tradition, and the intricate web of obligations that held their community together.

But they also knew, finally, that the love was real. And that knowledge—bittersweet and painful as it was—would have to be enough.

Chapter 6
Outside Threats

The town hall buzzed with a peculiar energy that unsettled Esther as she fidgeted on the hard wooden bench in Miracle Creek's community center. Surrounded by the familiar shapes of her father and sister, both clad in the humble garb of their faith, she felt like a fragile bird caught between two worlds—the one she cherished and the one that thrummed impatiently beyond the center's doors. The space swirled with voices and intentions, a turbulent undercurrent that left her heart fluttering with unease as the weight of the *Englisch* men's confidence loomed heavy in the air.

With each creak of the wooden benches, Esther shifted uncomfortably, the smooth fabric of her dress brushing against her skin in a reminder of how out of place she felt amidst the crispness of suits and polished shoes that flanked her on all sides.

She felt small here, a witness to a grand game unfolding—one that might hold the future of their community in the hands of men like Jacob Turner. A man of the Amish world, yet not entirely of it; someone with a foot in both camps. Although Esther knew the Amish could never truly leave someone behind—it was woven into their very being, in more ways than one, even when venturing into the *Englisch* world.

At the front of the hall stood Jacob, a stark figure with his tailored suit and bright tie, his confident posture radiating authority and purpose. He stood beside elaborate display boards, their glossy images depicting visions of opulence—a luxury hotel and shopping experience nestled in the heart of Amish Country.

As he spoke into the microphone, his voice echoed unnaturally through the room, reverberating against the walls in a manner that felt foreign to her ears.

"Ladies and gentlemen," Jacob began, his smile practiced and wide, "brothers and sisters… what I'm proposing here is nothing short of transformational. This development will bring unprecedented economic opportunity to your community while preserving—indeed, celebrating—the unique Amish heritage that makes this area so special."

Esther watched as several *Englisch* businessmen nodded approvingly from the side of the room, their phones and tablets glowing like strange modern hearth fires. But among her own people, the response was more measured —concerned glances exchanged, weathered hands gripping hat brims, a collective wariness settling over the Amish section like morning fog.

"The Yoder farm," Jacob continued, gesturing to a map that showed property lines in stark red and green, "with its prime location and creek access, represents the cornerstone of this vision. With the right development, we're talking about jobs, tourism revenue, and putting Miracle Creek on the map as a premier destination. Something that will benefit you all."

Esther's stomach tightened at the mention of the Yoder farm. She found herself searching the crowd for Eli, finally spotting him near the back, sitting alone. His posture was rigid, his face drawn with the weight of impossible decisions. She watched as he scribbled notes on a small pad, his jaw clenched tight.

Their eyes met across the crowded room, and in that brief moment, Esther saw the conflict raging within him— the farm that had been in his family for generations weighed against crushing debt, his grandmother's needs balanced against his ancestors' legacy, duty to the past warring with practical survival.

She wanted to go to him, to offer comfort or counsel, but Martha sat three rows ahead with her family, her back straight and proper, occasionally glancing back at Eli with an expression that was difficult to read—concern mixed with something that looked almost like calculation.

"Let me be clear," Jacob said, his voice taking on a tone of practiced sincerity. "I'm not here to destroy your way of life. I'm here to enhance it, to create opportunities for your children and grandchildren. The world is changing, friends. The question isn't whether that change will come, but whether you'll have a hand in shaping it."

A murmur rippled through the *Englisch* attendees—approval and excitement. But among the Amish, the reaction was decidedly different. Esther saw the older men shift uneasily, their expressions troubled. This wasn't just about land or money; it was about the very fabric of their existence.

As Jacob wrapped up his presentation to polite applause from the business crowd, Esther watched her father rise slowly from his seat. Daniel Troyer's weathered face was composed, but she could see the determination in his eyes as he made his way toward the front of the room.

The crowd quieted as Daniel reached the front, his simple clothing and untrimmed beard a stark contrast to Jacob's polished appearance. He turned to face the assembly, his hands clasped loosely in front of him, his voice calm but carrying a weight that made people lean forward to listen. His voice boomed into the mic.

"Thank you, Mr. Turner, for your presentation," Daniel began, his tone respectful but firm. "You speak of opportunity and progress, and I don't doubt your sincerity. But I must speak a word of caution to my own community."

He paused, his gaze sweeping across the Amish families gathered. "This land we stand on—the farms we tend, the fields we plow—these are not merely property to be bought and sold for profit. They are our heritage, purchased with the sweat and prayers of our forefathers who came to this country seeking freedom to worship and live according to our conscience."

Esther felt her throat tighten with emotion as her father continued. She saw heads nodding among the Amish families, saw the older generation settling into their seats with expressions of approval.

"When we sell our land," Daniel said, his voice growing more passionate, "we sell more than soil and timber. We sell the places where our children learned to walk, where our parents are buried, where generations have gathered for worship and fellowship. We sell our separation from the world, our ability to live simply and apart."

Jacob shifted uncomfortably, his polished smile wavering slightly. Several of the *Englisch* businessmen exchanged glances, clearly not having anticipated this kind of resistance.

"Mr. Turner speaks of change as inevitable," Daniel continued. "But we Amish have faced the pressure to change for over three hundred years. We have held fast to our principles not because we fear the future, but because we treasure what we have. Our way of life is not a museum piece for tourists to gawk at—it is our faith made visible, our commitment to community over individual gain, our trust in *Gott's* providence rather than man's schemes."

The room was utterly silent now, every eye fixed on Daniel. Esther felt tears prick her eyes as she watched her father defend not just land, but their very identity.

"I urge my brothers and sisters," Daniel said, his voice

softening but losing none of its intensity, "to think carefully before making decisions that cannot be unmade. The money Mr. Turner offers may seem like salvation from debt, like security for our families. But what profit is there in gaining the whole world if we lose our souls? If we lose our community? If we lose the very thing that makes us who we are?"

He turned to look at Jacob directly. "Mr. Turner, I thank you for your time and your offer. But I pray that any man considering selling his heritage will count the cost—not just in dollars, but in the things that cannot be measured or replaced."

As Daniel returned to his seat, the division in the room was palpable. The *Englisch* businessmen looked frustrated, their lucrative development suddenly complicated by moral and cultural concerns they hadn't anticipated. But among the Amish, there was a sense of solidarity, of renewed commitment to their values.

Esther watched as the meeting began to break up, families clustering together in quiet conversation. She saw Eli remain in his seat, his head bowed, the notepad clutched in his hands. Martha's father approached him, speaking in low tones, gesturing toward the display boards and then toward the door where Jacob stood chatting with potential investors.

The pressure on Eli was visible, almost tangible. His farm was the keystone of Jacob's development plan— without it, the entire project would likely collapse. And Eli's debts were real, his grandmother's needs genuine. Daniel's words had been true and powerful, but they didn't pay bills or put food on the table.

Esther longed to go to him, but Martha was already making her way to Eli's side, her hand possessive on his arm as she spoke quietly to him. The message was clear:

whatever decision Eli made, Martha would be part of it. She was his intended, his future wife, and that gave her a claim that Esther could never have.

As families began filing out of the community center, Esther found herself caught in the crowd, separated from her father and Mae. She was swept along with the flow toward the exit, and found herself emerging into the cool evening air just as Eli was climbing into his buggy.

Their eyes met again, and this time there was no crowd to buffer them, no distance to soften the impact. Eli looked torn, anguished, a man being pulled in too many directions at once.

Esther felt her feet carrying her toward him before she could think better of it. "Eli," she called softly.

He paused, one foot on the buggy step, his entire body tense. Martha stood a few feet away, speaking with her father, but her attention was clearly on Eli and Esther.

"You're actually considering it, aren't you?" Esther said, the words escaping before she could stop them. "Selling the farm. Selling your family's legacy."

Eli's jaw tightened, his eyes flashing with a mixture of pain and frustration. "Not all of us have the luxury of holding onto ideals when reality comes knocking."

The words stung, and Esther felt herself recoil. "By betraying everything our community stands for? Everything your father worked for?"

"My father left me with debts and a sick grandmother to care for," Eli shot back, his voice rising slightly despite his obvious effort at control.

Esther's voice trembled now with a mixture of hurt and frustration. "I can't understand the burden you carry. But you're considering selling our heritage for profit—"

"For survival," Eli interrupted. "There's a difference."

A small crowd was beginning to gather, drawn by the

tension between them. Esther saw Martha watching with sharp eyes, saw her own father emerge from the community center and pause, concern crossing his features. But she couldn't stop now, couldn't walk away from this conversation even though she knew she should.

"Eli," she said, softening her voice, trying to reach past his defensive walls. "Don't turn your back on us—on everything we've fought for."

"And if the bills come knocking and the debts suffocate me?" Eli challenged, frustration evident in every line of his body. "What do I do then, Esther? Hold tight to tradition and watch it all disappear? Watch my grandmother lose her home? Lose everything my family built?"

"You don't have to be alone in this," Esther urged, stepping closer despite the impropriety, despite the watching eyes. "Let us find a way to make it work without sacrificing who we are."

For a moment, something shifted in Eli's expression—a flicker of doubt, of longing, of hope that maybe there was another path. But then Martha appeared at his elbow, her presence a cold reminder of reality.

"Eli," Martha said quietly but firmly. "We should go. My father wants to discuss Jacob's kind offer with you."

The spell broke. Eli's face hardened again, the walls slamming back into place. "You don't understand the choices I'm facing," he said to Esther, but there was a note of uncertainty now, as if he were trying to convince himself as much as her.

"Neither do you," Esther replied softly, tears threatening. "This isn't just about survival; it's about our identity. Who will we become if we allow these decisions to unfold?"

The words hung in the air between them, weighted with all the things they couldn't say—about the betrothal that bound him, about the feelings that connected them, about the future that seemed to be slipping away from them both.

"I have to go," Eli said finally, his voice flat. He climbed into the buggy, and Martha followed, settling beside him with an expression of satisfaction barely concealed.

"Eli!" Esther called after him, but he was already urging the horse forward, unable or unwilling to meet her eyes again.

As the buggy pulled away, Esther stood in the gathering dusk, watching until it disappeared from view. She felt her father's hand on her shoulder, gentle and understanding.

"Come, *dochder*," Daniel said quietly. "It's time to go home."

Esther allowed herself to be led to their own buggy, but as she climbed in beside Mae, she couldn't resist one last glance back at the community center. Through the windows, she could see Jacob Turner still inside, surrounded by his business associates and Martha's father, no doubt strategizing how to overcome the resistance Daniel had stirred up.

The battle for their community's soul had only just begun, and Eli Yoder stood at the center of it—caught between the weight of his debts and the weight of his heritage, between the practical demands of survival and the spiritual demands of faith.

And somewhere in that complicated tangle, Esther knew, was their own story—two hearts that had finally recognized their connection only to find it threatened by forces far larger than themselves.

As their buggy rolled through the darkening countryside, Esther closed her eyes and whispered a prayer: "Lord, give him wisdom. Give him strength. And whatever happens, please don't let him lose himself in the process."

But even as she prayed, she felt the cold weight of fear

settling in her chest. Change was coming to Miracle Creek, whether they wanted it or not. The only question now was whether their community—and whether Eli—would survive it intact.

* * *

That night, Eli sat alone in his kitchen, the contract from Jacob Turner spread across the table before him. The numbers were staggering—enough to pay off every debt, to secure his grandmother's care for the rest of her life, to finally breathe without the crushing weight of financial ruin bearing down on him.

All he had to do was sell the land his grandfather had cleared with his own hands. Give up the fields his father had taught him to plow. Surrender the creek where he'd played as a boy and dreamed of bringing his own children someday. The creek the town was named after.

He thought of Esther's words: *Our way of life is more important than financial security.* Easy to say when you weren't drowning in debt. Easy to believe when you had choices.

But then he thought of the way she'd looked at him in the storage barn during the storm, the truth finally spoken between them after so many years of silence. How could he marry Martha when Esther's words echoed in his heart? How could he sell his heritage when doing so meant severing his connection to everything that had made him who he was?

But how could he not, when the alternative was losing everything anyway?

Eli dropped his head into his hands, the weight of seemingly impossible choices crushing down on him. Outside, the stars wheeled overhead, silent and distant, offering no answers to the questions that tormented him.

And somewhere across those dark fields, Esther lay

awake in her own bed, staring at the ceiling and wondering if the man she loved would choose survival over soul, if practicality would win over principle, if their community would fracture under the pressure of the modern world encroaching on their peaceful corner of Lancaster County.

The battle lines had been drawn, and tomorrow would bring new challenges. But tonight, they were both simply two people caught in the crossfire of change, hoping against hope that somehow, love and faith would be enough to see them through.

Chapter 7
Whispers and Warnings

The afternoon sun poured through the front windows of Albert King's General Store, illuminating dust motes that danced lazily in the warm light. The rich colors of the calico fabrics beckoned to Esther, each bolt a promise of creativity and inspiration, yet beneath her calm exterior lay the ever-looming specter of discontent, threads of unease stitching themselves tightly around her heart. Today marked the beginning of a new quilt commission—a chance for her artistry to breathe and flourish—yet the anticipation felt muted, tinged with an undercurrent of apprehension.

She moved to the fabric counter, her fingers gliding across the textured fabrics, savoring the familiar weight of each bolt, the soft cotton whispering secrets of patterns yet unwoven. The array of colors splashed across the table, each swatch a delicate promise of stories to be stitched into the quilt, and for a moment, Esther allowed herself to envision the finished piece: the way the colors would meld, the warmth radiating from the lovingly crafted squares, inviting the touch of generations to come.

Yet, the tranquil atmosphere of the store soon began to fray at the edges, her excitement muddied by the hushed tones filtering through the air, barely louder than the soft click of the storekeeper's fingers on the ledger as Albert tallied sales. At the next counter, she caught the familiar voices of Veronica Zook and Dorcas Hershberger, their presence an ever-watchful eye in her periphery.

"Did you hear about Eli Yoder?" Veronica's voice danced lightly at first, but then turned lower, the timbre charged with knowing significance. Esther felt her heart skip, her hands stilling over a bolt of deep blue fabric.

"What about him?" Dorcas replied, her tone pitched just loud enough to carry.

"That *Englisch* developer has made him quite an offer," Veronica continued, deliberately not lowering her voice despite Esther's obvious presence nearby. "Jacob Turner was seen at the Yoder farm twice this week. Some say Eli's seriously considering it."

Esther's fingers tightened on the fabric, the soft cotton suddenly feeling coarse against her palms.

"Well, the boy does have debts," Dorcas said, her voice carrying a note of sympathy tinged with judgment. "His father—God rest his soul—left things in quite a state. And with Mammi Yoder's recent illness…"

"Still," Veronica interjected, her tone sharpening, "selling one's heritage for *Englisch* money. What will folks say?"

"I know what Martha's father will say. His property borders the Yoders, so he is all for it, I should say. It will benefit them but unless Eli sells, the deal is off…"

Esther knew she should move away, should remove herself from this conversation that was clearly intended for her ears. But her feet remained rooted to the spot, her heart pounding as the women's words washed over her.

"And speaking of impropriety," Veronica said, her voice dropping to a conspiratorial whisper that somehow carried perfectly to where Esther stood, "I've heard some concerning things about certain unmarried women spending excessive time at the Yoder farm."

The words hit Esther like a physical blow. She felt heat flood her cheeks, shame and indignation warring within her chest.

"*Ach* now, Veronica," Dorcas said, though her tone lacked true censure. "Esther Troyer was caring for Mammi

Yoder during her illness. That's hardly—"

"*Ja. Soh*, Of course, of course," Veronica interrupted smoothly. "Christian charity and all that. But one does wonder if Martha Stoltzfus appreciates having another young woman so... involved with her intended husband's household affairs." She paused meaningfully. "Some unmarried women simply don't know their place."

Esther's hands trembled as she fumbled with the fabric bolts, her vision blurring with unshed tears. The cruelty of it—the twisting of her genuine care for Mammi Yoder into something sordid and inappropriate—felt like poison seeping into her veins.

"Martha has been very gracious about the whole situation," Dorcas observed. "Though I did hear her mention to the bishop that she hopes, once she and Eli are properly wed, there will be no 'confusion' about who manages the Yoder household."

The storekeeper, Albert King, appeared suddenly at Esther's elbow, his weathered face kind and understanding. His salt and pepper hair seemed to grow grayer every time Esther saw him. More salt and less pepper. "Don't pay them any mind," he whispered, placing a gentle hand on Esther's arm. "Some people have nothing better to do than stir up trouble where none exists."

But Esther could barely hear him over the roaring in her ears. She placed her fabric selections on the counter with shaking hands, counting out coins from her small purse with deliberate focus, determined not to let the watching women see how deeply their words had cut.

"*Denki*, Mr King," Esther managed, her voice steadier than she felt.

As she gathered her purchases and turned to leave, she felt the weight of Veronica and Dorcas's gazes following her. She kept her head high, her steps measured, refusing to give them the satisfaction of seeing her flee.

But once outside, the crisp autumn air hit her face like a splash of cold water, and Esther felt the tears she'd been holding back begin to slip free. She hurried toward her waiting buggy, clutching her fabric bundle against her chest like a shield.

How had everything become so tangled? She'd only wanted to help a sick woman, to use the healing knowledge her mother had passed down. But now her kindness had been twisted into scandal, her concern painted as improper pursuit of another woman's intended.

And Eli—poor Eli, caught between crushing debt and community expectation, between his heritage and his survival. No matter what choice he made, someone would judge him for it. If he sold to Jacob Turner, he'd be condemned as a traitor to their way of life. If he refused and lost the farm anyway, he'd be pitied as a fool who let pride destroy him.

Esther climbed into her buggy, her purchases forgotten on the seat beside her as she sat gripping the reins with white-knuckled hands. The sun that had seemed so warm earlier now felt harsh and exposing, illuminating every flaw, every mistake, every impossible tangle of her situation.

A shadow fell across her buggy, and Esther looked up to find Daniel standing beside her, concern etched across his weathered features. She hadn't even noticed him approaching.

"I saw you come out the store," her *datt* said gently. "Are you well, *dochder?*"

Esther opened her mouth to assure him she was fine, but the kindness in his eyes undid her. A sob escaped before she could stop it, and then her father's arms were around her, solid and safe, as she cried against his shoulder.

"I heard them," Daniel said quietly when her tears had

subsided to hiccups. "The Zook and Hershberger women. Their tongues are sharper than any blade."

"They think I was inappropriate," Esther whispered. "That I was pursuing Eli when he's promised to Martha. But I was only trying to help Mammi Yoder, *Datt.* I swear it."

"I know that, child," Daniel soothed, his hand gentle on her back. "And so does anyone with sense. But gossip rarely concerns itself with truth."

He helped her settle back onto the buggy seat, then stood beside her, his expression thoughtful. "Esther, I need to speak with you about something. There's been...a proposal."

Esther's heart sank. She knew that tone, that careful way her father had of approaching difficult subjects.

"Aaron Lapp," Daniel continued, "a widower from Peace Haven in Ohio. Bishop Lapp's kin. He's been corresponding with me these past few weeks. He's looking for a wife, someone to help him raise his young children. He's heard of your gentle nature and your skill with healing from Bishop Lapp."

"Datt, nee!" Esther breathed, horror washing over her.

"Hear me out," Daniel said, his voice firm but kind. "Aaron is a *gut* man, a devout man. His children need a mother. And perhaps..." He paused, choosing his words carefully. "Perhaps some distance from Miracle Creek would be good for you right now. A chance to start fresh, away from wagging tongues and... complicated situations."

Esther understood what he wasn't saying. Her father was trying to protect her—from gossip, from heartbreak, from the impossible situation with Eli. Aaron Lapp represented a respectable escape, a way to salvage her reputation and find purpose at the same time.

But the thought of leaving—of never seeing Eli again,

of abandoning her home and her community—felt like death.

"I need time to think," Esther said, her voice small.

"Of course," Daniel agreed. "But Esther, you must understand—things are becoming complicated here. The community is watching. Martha has made her concerns known to the bishop. And Eli Yoder..." He trailed off, shaking his head. "That young man is wrestling with demons. I don't envy him. The choices he faces would break a lesser man."

"I know," Esther whispered.

"Whatever decision you make," Daniel said, "know that I want only your happiness. But happiness and wisdom don't always align, *dochder*. Sometimes we must choose the path that protects our hearts and our reputations, even if it's not the path we'd prefer."

He patted her hand once more, then stepped back. "Come home when you're ready. Your aunt Rebecca is visiting this evening. She'll want to see you."

Esther watched her father walk away, his broad shoulders carrying the weight of community leadership and fatherly concern in equal measure. Then she urged her horse forward, letting the gentle rhythm of hooves on packed earth carry her away from the store, away from the whispers, away from the impossible choices that seemed to multiply with each passing day.

But she couldn't outrun the truth: her world was shifting, foundations she'd thought solid crumbling beneath her feet. And somewhere in the chaos, Eli Yoder was facing his own impossible decisions—decisions that would shape not just his future, but hers as well.

* * *

The soft glow of lantern light danced in the Troyer family dining room, illuminating the worn oak table scattered with remnants of supper. Esther moved with practiced grace, helping Mae clear the dishes, each click of porcelain punctuating the familiarity of home. Yet, beneath the warmth of the gathered family, a quiet tension simmered—an undercurrent of worry that pulled at her heart like the weight of unspoken secrets.

Aunt Rebecca sat at the far end of the table, her sharp eyes observing Esther with an intensity that made the younger woman's skin prickle with awareness. Esther had known from the moment her aunt arrived that this evening would bring more than just a simple family visit.

"You missed a fork, Esther!" Mae chimed, her playful voice breaking through Esther's thoughts. The younger sister leaned over the table, her wild hair cascading around her shoulders beneath her *kapp* as she giggled, her carefree spirit a refreshing contrast to Esther's swirling emotions.

Across the table, Daniel continued to read from the Bible, his voice steady and grounding, while the occasional hum of assent punctuated the stillness. It was a ritual Esther cherished—a moment of connection that fortified their family bonds. She couldn't help but steal glances toward her father, the comforting cadence of his voice enveloping the room in warmth.

When Daniel concluded the reading, they joined hands for evening prayer. Esther bowed her head, but the words of gratitude felt hollow on her lips. How could she be grateful when her heart was breaking? How could she trust in *Gott's* plan when it seemed to be leading her away from everything—and everyone—she loved?

"Amen," the family chorused, and Esther lifted her head to find Aunt Rebecca's eyes fixed on her.

"Come help me in the kitchen, Esther," her aunt said,

her voice pleasant but leaving no room for argument.

In the kitchen, away from Mae and the comfort of her father's presence, Esther felt suddenly exposed. Aunt Rebecca moved about with efficient purpose, arranging dishes that didn't need arranging, her silence deliberate and loaded.

"Your father tells me you've been visiting the Yoder farm frequently," Rebecca finally said, not looking at Esther as she spoke.

"Mammi Yoder was very ill," Esther replied, keeping her voice steady. "Someone needed to care for her"

"And it had to be you?" Rebecca turned now, her expression pointed. "An unmarried woman, spending hours alone with a betrothed man?"

"His grandmother was there," Esther protested. "And I was never—"

"Esther," her aunt interrupted, her tone sharp, "you know how gossip travels in our community. It has even reached Hope Valley, for goodness sake. I heard talk at the quilting circle there! Folks notice how often you visit that farm. They notice the way you look at Eli Yoder. They notice the way he looks at you."

Esther's breath caught. "I don't know what you mean."

"Don't play coy with me, child," Rebecca said, her voice softening slightly but losing none of its intensity. "I didn't come down in the last rain shower. I knew your mother well enough to see her spirit in you. She had that same stubborn heart, that same foolish romanticism. And do you know what it cost her?"

Esther stiffened. "My mother—"

"Your mother waited too long to speak her heart to your father," Rebecca said bluntly. "She nearly lost him to another woman because she was too afraid of what people would think, too worried about propriety."

The words struck Esther like a slap. She'd never known this about her parents, never imagined their love story had been anything but simple and straightforward.

"But you and she, alike as you are do not face the same situation. In your case, Eli Yoder is already promised to Martha Stoltzfus. Eli's honor—not to mention his financial situation—binds him to that commitment."

"I know that," Esther whispered, tears threatening.

"Do you?" Rebecca challenged. "Because from where I stand, you're clinging to impossible hopes that will only break your heart further." She paused, then delivered the words Esther had been dreading. "Aaron Lapp is a good man, Esther. A godly man. His children need a mother, and he can provide you with a respectable home and a fresh start."

"I don't love him," Esther said, the words escaping before she could stop them. "I don't even *know* him!"

"Love," Rebecca scoffed, though not unkindly. "Love is what you build through shared work and shared faith and shared purpose. This foolish notion of romantic love—it's a luxury, Esther, not a necessity. Better to marry a good man you respect than to waste away pining for one you can never have."

"Is that what you did?" Esther asked, a note of defiance entering her voice. "Married for practicality?"

Rebecca's face softened, something like old pain flickering in her eyes. "*Ja,*" she said simply. "And I've had a *gut* life because of it. Not the life I dreamed of as a girl, perhaps, but a solid one. A faithful one."

She reached out and took Esther's hand. "Sometimes the path of wisdom is not the path we'd choose with our hearts. But it's the path that keeps us whole."

Esther pulled her hand away, frustration and heartbreak warring in her chest. "*Ach,* you don't understand—"

"I understand better than you know," Rebecca said firmly. "I understand that you care for Eli Yoder. I understand that he cares for you as well. But I also understand that feelings alone cannot overcome the bonds of betrothal, the weight of debt, or the expectations of community. You're tilting at windmills, child, and you'll only hurt yourself—and him—in the process."

Before Esther could respond, a knock at the kitchen door startled them both. Daniel appeared in the doorway, his expression troubled.

"Esther," he said quietly, "Eli Yoder is here. He says he needs to return something to you."

Esther's heart leaped into her throat. Behind her, she felt Rebecca's disapproving silence like a physical weight. She followed her father to the front porch, where Eli stood in the gathering darkness, a small bundle in his hands.

It was a pie plate—one Esther had brought to the Yoder farm days ago with a meal for Mammi Yoder. She'd completely forgotten about it in the chaos of everything that had followed.

"I've been meaning to return this," Eli said, his voice formal, his eyes not quite meeting hers. "*Denki* for the kindness to my grandmother."

Esther took the plate, her fingers brushing his briefly, sending electricity through her despite the awkwardness of the moment. "How is she feeling now?" she asked, desperate to prolong this interaction, to find some excuse to speak with him beyond pleasantries.

"Much better," Eli replied, finally meeting her gaze. "Thanks to you."

"Thanks to *Gott*." Esther pointed heavenward and smiled.

They stood in stilted silence, the weight of everything unsaid hanging between them like morning mist. Esther was acutely aware of her father standing just inside the doorway, of Aunt Rebecca no doubt listening from the kitchen, of the impropriety of this extended conversation on her family's porch.

But she couldn't let him leave without asking. "Eli, about the farm—have you made a decision about Jacob Turner's offer?"

Something shuttered in Eli's expression. "That's not really your concern, Esther."

The formal distance in his voice cut her more deeply than any harsh word could have. This was Eli protecting himself, building walls between them, doing what he thought was honorable even though it was destroying them both.

"Of course," Esther said, her voice brittle. "Forgive me for overstepping."

Eli's jaw clenched, and for a moment she thought he might say something more, might break through the formality to speak truth. But then his shoulders sagged slightly, defeat settling over him like a cloak.

"I should go," he said. "Martha is expecting me."

It was the first time he'd mentioned Martha's name directly to Esther, and the deliberate reminder of his betrothal felt like a door closing. This was Eli trying to do the right thing, trying to honor his commitments even as his heart pulled him in another direction.

"*Gudi nacht*, Eli," Esther whispered.

He turned and walked to his buggy, and Esther stood on the porch watching him leave, the forgotten pie plate clutched in her hands like a talisman of all she'd lost.

As Eli drove away into the darkness, his hands tight on the reins, he made a decision. He would honor his commitment to Martha. He would try—truly try—to build a life with her. And he would let Esther Troyer go, even though it felt like cutting out his own heart.

Behind him, on the porch, Esther finally turned to go inside, where Aunt Rebecca waited with more arguments for practicality, for Aaron Lapp, for leaving Miracle Creek behind and starting fresh somewhere her heart wouldn't constantly break.

That night, two people were caught in the cruel machinery of trying to do the honorable thing even as it destroyed them. And in the darkness between their two farms, the impossible distance seemed to grow wider with each passing moment.

Chapter 8
A Revelation

In the dim embrace of the Yoder barn, shafts of sunlight poured through the weathered cracks in the wood, igniting motes of dust that swirled in a lazy dance. Eli Yoder moved among the remnants of scattered hay bales, his heart thrumming against the stillness, a pulse of frustration building in his chest as he searched for the missing harness strap. The barn, with its familiar scents of earth and work, felt like a refuge, yet today it closed in around him, mirroring the storm of thoughts and unspoken words that tangled his mind.

The remnants of their recent storm cleanup littered the floor, bales overturned in haste, a chaotic disarray that seemed to reflect the turmoil twisting within him. He pushed back a pile of hay, wincing at the strain in his shoulders, muscles clenching as memories of the storm swirled around him like shadows. The weight of Esther's presence lingered in the corners of his mind, urging him to uncover the harness strap he had hastily misplaced during the frenzy.

His fingers slid over coarse fibers, anxiety sparking as he thought back to the closeness they had shared in this very loft during the thunderstorm—that charged moment when truth had finally broken free between them, only to be crushed again by the weight of duty and misunderstanding.

"Think of something else," Eli muttered to himself, but the refrain of their connection was all-consuming. Each movement of his hands through the hay seemed to unfurl strands of longing and possibility, deepening the ache that lay heavy in his chest. The outside world, vibrant with sounds of laughter and calls from the fields, faded to a distant echo, pushing his focus deeper inward.

Shifting a particularly large bale near where he and Esther had sat during the storm, Eli's calloused fingers brushed against something solid. He paused, blinking against the shafts of sunlight pooling around it, and pulled it free—a small Bible, slightly scuffed but sturdy, clearly well-loved.

His pulse quickened as he flipped it open, eyes catching the name written in careful, neat script inside the cover: *Esther Troyer.*

Eli's fingers trembled as he held the Bible, the name *Esther Troyer* still vivid in his mind. He stopped at the story of Hagar. He read the story of Hagar again, each word pressing into him like a mirror he could not look away from.

Gott had promised Abraham and Sarah a child. But when the promise seemed slow to come, they took matters into their own hands, arranging for concubine Hagar to bear a son, Ishmael, for Abraham instead. Logical. Practical. Reasonable. Especially considering Sarah's advanced years. The done thing even at the time. And yet the result had been far from blessed: jealousy, bitterness, conflict, consequences that stretched across generations.

A chill ran down Eli's spine. How easy it was to think he was doing the right thing, to act in accordance with duty and propriety, and yet miss the will of God entirely. By agreeing to marry Martha, was he about to follow the same path? To act in what seemed like the sensible course— honoring betrothal, maintaining appearances, fulfilling obligation—while ignoring the voice of *Gott* in his heart? Was he about to birth an Ishmael instead of an Isaac, a life born of human planning rather than divine promise?

The barn was quiet, the shafts of sunlight catching dust motes that hung in the air like tiny spirits. He felt the weight of his choices pressing on him. Every thought of

Martha, of duty, of following the path laid before him by family and tradition, suddenly felt heavy, constricting. And Esther—her name, her presence, her very soul—rose before him like a standard he could not lower. Could he truly claim to honor *Gott* if he chose a path that would deny the love he knew in his heart, the voice he felt in quiet moments, whispering that this was not right?

His hands shook, closing the Bible carefully as though even the act of holding it too tightly might shatter him. He realized now that this was *Gott* speaking, not through thunder or fire, but through story, through reflection, through the still, convicting voice in his own conscience. Every beat of his heart echoed with the warning: choices made from obligation, from fear, or from practicality, without listening to *Gott,* could bring strife instead of blessing.

Eli pressed his palms to his face, the realization burning through him. He could not take the easy path, not now, not ever. To marry Martha out of duty, to follow the expected path without regard for *Gott's* guidance in his heart, would be to follow Abraham's error—not Abraham himself, but the human plan that ran ahead of God's promise. And what of Esther? What if he silenced that truth, as he had for so long, only to live with the consequences of a choice made without faith?

The barn was still, and Eli's breath came in ragged pulls. He had always known the difference between right and easy, but now it was sharper, more immediate. To follow *Gott* meant courage. To obey meant sacrifice. And suddenly, the Hagar story was no longer distant history. It was a mirror. It was a warning. It was a voice—convicting, unrelenting, impossible to ignore.

"Oh, Esther," Eli breathed into the empty barn. How easy it was, he thought, to try to take control—to act in what seemed the most sensible way—only to find that human decisions, even made with the best intentions, could bring pain instead of blessing. What had he taken into his own hands? What might he have done in his desire to protect, to fix, to act?

Eli sank down onto a hay bale, the Bible clutched in his hands, as the full weight of his blindness crashed down upon him. All this time—all these wasted years—because he'd overheard one conversation taken out of context. Because he'd been too proud, too hurt, too foolish to simply ask her the truth.

And now? Her confession in this place had been that she loved him. Had always loved him. Still loved him, even knowing he was promised to another.

The barn suddenly felt too small, the air too thin. Eli shot to his feet, pacing between the hay bales, the bible in his hands.

"Eli? Are you in here?"

The voice from the barn entrance froze him in place. His grandmother appeared in the doorway, moving slowly but steadily, her recovery from pneumonia nearly complete.

"Mammi," Eli said, quickly tucking the Bible into his pocket. "You shouldn't be up and about—"

"I'm fine," she said dismissively, making her way toward him with the determined shuffle of someone who refused to be treated as an invalid. Her sharp eyes took in his disheveled appearance, the hay in his hair, the guilty expression on his face. "What's troubling you, son?"

"Nothing, I just—I was looking for the harness strap and—"

"Eli." His grandmother's voice was gentle but firm. "I've known you since the day you were born. Don't insult my intelligence by pretending everything is fine when you're clearly falling apart."

The simple kindness in her voice, the unconditional acceptance, broke something loose in Eli. He sank back onto the hay bale, his head in his hands.

"Now you know Esther loves you," Mammi said simply, lowering herself onto an adjacent bale with a soft grunt.

Eli's head snapped up. "You knew?"

"Of course I knew," Mammi replied, a hint of exasperation in her tone. "A blind man could see it. The way she looked at you when she thought no one was watching. The care she put into healing me—yes, because she's a good Christian woman, but also because it meant she could be near you." She shook her head. "And the way you look at her, like she's the sun and you're a flower that's been in shadow too long."

"But—the betrothal—"

"Is a mistake," Mammi said bluntly.

"The contracts are signed," Eli said desperately. "Breaking the betrothal would shame both families. Martha doesn't deserve that."

"Martha deserves a husband who loves her," Mammi countered. "Do you think she doesn't know? Do you think she can't feel that your heart isn't in this?" She reached out and took his hand. "You're trying to do the honorable thing, and I love you for it. But sometimes honor demands that we tell the truth, even when it's difficult. Especially when it's difficult.

"Eli, you need to understand something. If you marry Martha while loving Esther, you'll be living a lie. Every day. Every night. Every time you look at your wife and wish she were someone else. Is that the honorable path? Is that fair to Martha, to yourself, to the children you might have?"

The truth of her words settled over him like a weight. He'd been so focused on not breaking his commitment to Martha that he hadn't considered how much more he'd be breaking by keeping it—the daily betrayal of loving someone else, the slow death of hope, the bitter poison of regret that would seep into everything he touched. It's not like he had not prayed that *Gott* would remove his feelings, enabling him to love Martha as he should. But those feelings had never come.

And now he knew it was human will and not *Gott's* will. And that tore at him.

"What do I do?" Eli asked, his voice breaking.

"You go to Esther," Mammi said firmly. "You lay your heart bare, and you let her make her own choice. Maybe she'll choose to wait while you figure out how to honorably end things with Martha. Maybe she won't. But at least you'll both know where you stand."

"And Martha?"

"Martha deserves honesty too," Mammi said. "She deserves to know that your heart belongs to another, that this betrothal was built on trying to act rightly rather than your own desires. It will hurt her, *ja*. But would you rather hurt her now, or hurt her worse by marrying her while loving someone else? And as for the farm… well, *Gott* has a way of coming *gut* just when we need it. Not always with what we want but with what we need."

Eli nodded slowly, the path forward beginning to crystallize in his mind. It wouldn't be easy. There would be scandal, disappointed expectations, complicated conversations with both families. But Mammi was right— he couldn't keep living this lie. Mammi's timing was perfect. *Gott's* timing was perfect.

"There's something else you should know," Mammi said, her expression growing more serious. "Esther's father was here yesterday while you were in the fields. Esther is leaving for Ohio today."

The words hit Eli like a punch to the gut. *"Today?"*

"He thought you should know," Mammi said gently.

Eli shot to his feet, the small Bible clutched in his hand, decision crystallizing into action. "I have to go. I have to see her before—"

"Then go," Mammi said, waving him toward the door.

Eli barely heard her as he burst from the barn into the bright afternoon sunlight. His fastest horse was already in the paddock, and his hands worked with practiced efficiency as he threw on the saddle and bridle, every movement driven by urgent desperation.

As he swung into the saddle, he caught sight of Martha's buggy turning into the lane. His heart sank—she was coming for her regular afternoon visit, no doubt with more wedding plans to discuss, more decisions to make about a future that felt increasingly like a noose tightening around his neck.

But he couldn't face her right now. Not before he'd spoken to Esther. Not before he'd tried to untangle this impossible knot.

"Tell her I had to go into town!" Eli called to one of the farmhands as he urged his horse into a gallop. "Tell her— tell her I'll call on her tomorrow!"

He didn't wait to see if the message was received. The horse thundered down the lane, hooves kicking up dust, carrying him toward the Troyer farm and the conversation that would determine the course of the rest of his life.

Behind him, Martha climbed down from her buggy, watching with narrowed eyes as Eli disappeared down the road. Her jaw tightened, a calculating expression crossing her features. She'd felt his distance growing, sensed his heart pulling away even as he tried to honor his commitments.

And she had a very good idea where he was going in such desperate haste.

She sighed. Jacob Turner would not be happy if the deal didn't go through. It all hung on Eli.

* * *

The road stretched before Eli like a ribbon of possibility and terror. His heart hammered in his chest, keeping time with the pounding of his horse's hooves. Esther's Bible burned in his pocket like a brand.

The miles passed in a blur of autumn fields and familiar landmarks. The old oak at Miller's Crossing. The covered bridge where he and Esther had played as children. Each sight reminded him of shared history, of a connection that had been there all along, waiting for them to be brave enough to acknowledge it.

As he crested the final hill before the Troyer farm, Eli's stomach dropped. In the yard below, he could see the family wagon already loaded with trunks and supplies, the horses in harness, Daniel checking the wheels with the careful attention of someone preparing for a long journey.

He was too late. They were leaving. Right now.

"*Nee!*" Eli shouted, spurring his horse down the hill with reckless speed. But even as he raced, the wagon pulled away, gaining distance with every frantic beat of his horse's hooves.

He urged the animal faster, closing the gap as best he could—but a loose stone sent the horse stumbling, and a startled neighbor's mare bolted across the road, forcing him to swerve. Precious seconds slipped away, and when he recovered, the wagon was already rounding a bend, disappearing behind the trees.

By the time he reached the Troyer farmyard, the wagon had vanished. He tore across the fields, hoping to catch a glimpse of them on the road, but it was too late. Esther was gone.

He pulled his horse to a halt, sitting in the middle of the empty road, chest heaving, hands shaking on the reins. The dust from the wagon's wheels hung in the air, settling slowly like his shattered hopes.

Too late. He was too late.

Esther was gone, headed to Ohio and Aaron Lapp, carrying her love for Eli locked in her heart like a secret that would slowly poison her with each passing day. And he was still here, trapped by honor and duty and the crushing weight of his own mistakes.

Eli bent forward in the saddle and for the first time since his father's death, he wept—for lost time, for wasted chances, for two hearts that had finally found each other only to be torn apart by circumstances beyond their control.

But even as despair threatened to overwhelm him, a stubborn spark of determination kindled in his chest. She loved him. And he loved her—had always loved her, even when he'd tried to convince himself otherwise.

He would have ridden after her, all the way to Ohio if he were free to, but he wasn't. Mammi needed him. His animals needed him. She was frail and entirely dependent on his care. He could not abandon her—not for a chase fueled by longing, not even for Esther.

By the time he reached the train station, heart pounding, sweat on his brow, the whistle had already sounded. The train that would carry Esther away was gone, its smoke trailing into the distance. He stood on the platform, helpless, his heart sinking. Duty and love were warring inside him, and for the first time in years, he understood the bitter weight of responsibility. He could follow his heart—or he could do what was right. And the right choice, as cruel as it felt, was to stay.

A month, Daniel had said to Mammi. They'd be gone a

month.

Eli straightened in the saddle, wiping his eyes with the back of his hand. A month. He had a month to figure out how to honorably end his betrothal to Martha, to settle his debts without selling his soul—or his land—to Jacob Turner, to prove to Esther and to himself that some things were worth fighting for, even when the fight seemed impossible.

He turned his horse and headed back toward home, the bible safe in his pocket.

"Wait for me, Esther," he whispered into the gathering dusk. "Just wait for me."

Chapter 9
Miles Apart

The Troyer family dining room in Peace Haven, Ohio, wrapped around Esther like a thick quilt, the warm glow of oil lamps casting flickering shadows against the plain walls. Each lamp threw soft light over the long wooden table, richly laden with simple yet hearty fare—freshly baked bread, steaming bowls of vegetable stew, and a pie cooling on the windowsill. Faces glowed in the amber light, some familiar with laughter and smiles, while others remained cautiously curious, glancing at her from beneath lowered lashes.

Esther found herself at the center of attention, yet a part of her felt as if she were looking through a window rather than sitting at the dinner table. Aaron Lapp, with his neatly trimmed beard and kind eyes, sat opposite her, exuding a warmth that should have been comforting but instead struck a chord of awkwardness deep within her.

"So, Esther, I heard you do quite a bit of quilting," he said, his tone friendly yet probing, as he ladled generous portions of stew into bowls for his children—eight-year-old Mary and six-year-old Joseph, both watching her with wide, hopeful eyes.

"Yes, I've been making quilts since I was a girl," Esther replied, her fingers fidgeting with the edge of her napkin, twisting the fabric into delicate folds. The gesture felt almost instinctual, a means to calm the fluttering anxiety tightening her chest as the focus settled squarely on her. She offered a polite smile but found herself unable to meet his gaze fully, her thoughts drifting toward the distant horizon, where home felt more like a fading dream than a tangible reality.

As Aaron continued to share his own experience with

woodworking, mentioning the intricacies of crafting furniture for their family, Esther managed to engage, nodding and responding with polite phrases. Yet the sound of his voice felt distant, a mere echo as her mind wandered back to Lancaster County—to Eli.

"Mary here has been wanting to learn to quilt," Aaron said warmly, drawing Esther's attention back to the present. "Perhaps you could teach her while you're visiting?"

Mary's face lit up with excitement, her small hands clasping together. "Really? Would you, Miss Esther?"

The child's enthusiasm pierced through Esther's melancholy, touching something tender in her heart. "I'd be happy to," she said, managing a genuine smile. "We could start with a simple pattern—perhaps a nine-patch square?"

"Can I help too?" Joseph piped up, not wanting to be left out.

"Everyone can help," Esther assured him, and for a moment, the weight on her chest lightened. These children had lost their mother. They needed care, guidance, love. Perhaps that was purpose enough, even if her heart ached for someone else.

As dinner continued, Esther observed the family dynamic—Aaron's patient attention to his children, the way Mary tried to be helpful beyond her years, how Joseph looked at Esther with an almost desperate hope, as if she might be the answer to prayers he was too young to articulate.

"After dinner, I'd like to show you my woodworking shop," Aaron proposed, the ease in his demeanor suggesting an earnest desire to connect. "I've been working on a hope chest for Mary—for when she's older, of course. Perhaps you could help me decide on the design for the lid."

"Oh, um, that would be lovely," Esther managed, though her heart wasn't in the words. She felt the gentle pressure of expectation settling around her like an invisible net—Aaron's hopes, his children's needs, her aunt's matchmaking, her father's desire to protect her reputation.

Everyone wanted something from her. Everyone except the one person whose wants might have aligned with her own. Or more like he wanted it but was trapped by duty and obligation.

* * *

Later that evening, after the children had been tucked into bed and the household had settled into quiet, Esther found herself drawn to the small creek that meandered behind the Troyer property. It reminded her of the creek that ran through Eli's farm.

The evening air was cool against her skin, carrying the scent of approaching winter and the whisper of water over stones.

Settling on a smooth stone at the creek's edge, Esther bowed her head and closed her eyes, seeking the presence of *Gott* in the quiet.

"Dear Lord," she whispered, her voice catching, "I don't know what You want from me anymore. I thought I was meant to care for Mammi Yoder, but that led me deeper into heartache. I thought maybe You were showing me a path with Eli, but that door seems closed and locked. And now I'm here, and these wonderful children need a mother, and Aaron is a *gut* man who could give me a respectable life, but..."

Her voice broke, tears slipping down her cheeks to fall into the creek below, mingling with the flowing water. "But I don't want it! My heart is still back in Lancaster County.

My heart is still with a man I can never have. How do I move forward when every step feels like walking away from the life I was meant to live? Is that selfish of me?"

"Everyone says it cannot be. But is the 'done thing' always your will? If Eli is not meant for me, then *you*, you please take away this ache," Esther prayed, her hands clasped so tightly her knuckles showed white. "Take away this longing so I can give my heart fully to whatever life You have planned whoever that is with. But Lord, if there's any possibility—any chance that You're making a way for us—parting the waters that surround us...."

She thought of Scripture, of the verses her mother had loved: "Trust in the Lord with all thine heart; and lean not unto thine own understanding. In all thy ways acknowledge Him, and He shall direct thy paths."

But which path? How could she trust when every direction seemed to lead to heartbreak?

Esther picked up a stick from beside the creek and began drawing in the soft, wet earth—patterns that came naturally to her fingers, the same designs she'd traced a thousand times in fabric. Diamonds and stars, interlocking circles, the geometric beauty that brought order to chaos.

As she worked, her mind turned over the events like a stone polished smooth by water. The misunderstanding that had started everything—Eli overhearing her deny her feelings out of embarrassment. The betrothal to Martha arranged by fathers, built on practicality rather than love. The storm in the barn when truth had finally broken free between them, only to be interrupted before it could fully bloom.

And now this—exile to Ohio, Aaron Lapp's gentle courtship, the pressure to choose a safe path even as her heart cried out for the dangerous one.

"I surrendered Eli to You," Esther whispered into the

gathering darkness. "I gave him up, told You I would accept whatever plan You had for me. But Lord, if that was Your will, why does it still hurt so much? Why does my heart refuse to surrender while my mind knows it must?"

Esther remained by the creek until the stars emerged overhead, glittering like promises or warnings—she couldn't tell which. Finally, shivering with cold, she gathered her shoes and made her way back to the farmhouse, her prayers still apparently unanswered but her heart somehow steadier.

Tomorrow would bring more time with Mary and Joseph, more gentle attention from Aaron, more pressure to see the wisdom in choosing the practical path. But tonight, under the stars that shone on both Peace Haven and Miracle Creek, Esther allowed herself to hope—just for a moment—that somehow, impossibly, God was making a way where there seemed to be none.

* * *

Meanwhile, back in Miracle Creek, Eli stood alone in the cornfield behind his farmhouse, the stalks rustling around him like whispers. The evening sun painted everything gold, but the beauty felt hollow without Esther there to see it.

"Lord," Eli prayed, his voice rough with emotion, "I don't want to be an Abraham doing the wrong thing but I don't know how to fix this. I don't know how to end things with Martha without hurt and shame. I don't know how to keep the farm without selling my soul to Jacob Turner. I don't know how to make any of this right."

He thought of Esther by now settled into the Troyer household, meeting Aaron's children, perhaps already beginning to imagine a life there. The thought made his chest tight with something that felt like panic.

"Give me wisdom," Eli continued, his hands clenched at his sides. "Give me courage. And Lord, if there's any way —any path forward that doesn't require me to betray either my word or my heart—please show me. Because right now, I can't see it."

As the sun sank below the horizon, Eli made a decision. Tomorrow, he would speak with Martha. Not to break the betrothal immediately—he owed her more respect than that—but to begin the difficult conversation.

And then he would find a way to reach Esther, to let her know that he was fighting for a chance—however slim— that they might find their way back to each other.

The road ahead would be difficult, filled with hurt feelings and disappointed expectations and the judgment of a community that valued tradition and propriety above all else. But as Eli ran his thumb over Esther's handwritten name one more time in the inside cover of her Bible, he knew with absolute certainty that she was worth it.

Some things were worth fighting for, even when the fight seemed impossible. Some loves were worth pursuing, even when the path was unclear. And some truths, once spoken, couldn't be unspoken—they could only be honored or betrayed.

Eli chose honor. But this time, honoring his heart rather than merely his obligations. Honouring *Gott* above man.

As darkness fell over the cornfield, he whispered into the night, hoping somehow his words would carry across the miles to where Esther sat by her own water, seeking her own answers:

"Wait for me, Esther. I'm coming for you. I don't know how yet, but I swear I'll find a way."

And in Peace Haven, Ohio, as Esther finally made her way to bed in the small guest room of the Troyer house, she felt an inexplicable warmth settle over her heart—not quite hope, not quite peace, but something like the memory of summer sun after a long, cold winter.

Perhaps, she thought as sleep finally claimed her, perhaps some prayers were answered not with words but with feelings, not with clarity but with the courage to keep believing even in the darkness.

Tomorrow would bring its own challenges, its own choices. But tonight, under the same stars, two hearts beat in synchronized longing, separated by miles but connected by something stronger than distance—the truth finally spoken, finally known, finally impossible to deny.

Chapter 10
The Letter

In the quaint corner of the Troyer home, the afternoon sun streamed through the window, illuminating the busy fingers of eight-year-old Mary as she wrestled with the needle. Esther watched with a soft smile, her heart swelling with fondness and patience. Here, amid the chaos of fabric and laughter, she found herself drawn into the comfort of creativity, even while the shadow of uncertainty loomed.

"Hold the fabric like this," Esther gently instructed, demonstrating how to grip the cloth between small hands. She leaned in closer, aware of the little girl's fumbled attempts as the needle dangled awkwardly in Mary's grasp, frustration swirling in the air like wisps of steam from the kettle simmering nearby. "Just like this—see? It's a simple stitch," she encouraged, her voice soothing as she deftly threaded the needle through the delicate quilt square.

With a determined nod, Mary mimicked her movements, brows furrowing in concentration. "It's not fair! The needle is too slippery!" she exclaimed, her eyes glistening with a mixture of frustration and resolve, the innocent outrage a reminder of the carefree days of youth.

A chuckle bubbled up within Esther, a lightness that transported her back to her own childhood—hours spent curled up beside her mother, tracing the fabric patterns as they quilted under the summer sun.

"You'll get the hang of it," she promised, running a gentle finger across the seam they were working on. "Sometimes it takes a little practice. Besides, you have me to help you."

"I want to make the best quilt ever!" Mary declared with fierce determination, the spark of ambition igniting in her hazel eyes. As she struggled, Esther's heart swelled, watching the girl's little fingers fight to tame the needle. There was beauty in the attempt, in the innocence that brushed against the hard edges of reality; moments like these carried with them the warmth of tradition, the essence of connection woven into every stitch.

As Mary pulled the fabric taut, the door swung open, revealing Aaron's unmarried *schwester*, Hannah. A cheerful smile adorning Hannah's face as she entered with a stack of envelopes cradled in her arms. "The day's mail just arrived," she said, her voice bright as morning sunlight.

With each step closer, the atmosphere shifted—an undeniable tension filled the air as Esther caught sight of the familiar penmanship on one of the envelopes. Her heart sank, recognition washing over her like an unexpected tide. It was Eli's handwriting, distinctive and bold, a reminder of the world she had left behind—tied tightly to every unspoken word lingering between them.

"Look, it's a letter for you!" Hannah exclaimed, oblivious to the whirlwind of emotions churning within Esther. As if in slow motion, Esther's fingers froze mid-stitch, her mind racing with thoughts she couldn't voice. Pushing the memories of their shared moments to the back of her mind, she cleared her throat.

"I—um, I need to check on something. Excuse me for a moment," Esther stammered, casting a quick glance at Mary's confused expression before retreating toward the guest bedroom, the envelope clutched tightly in her trembling hands. The door clicked softly behind her, the sound muffled against the swirl of her inner thoughts as she paced the small space, anxiety tightening its grip around her.

The room was dimly lit, dust motes caught in the shafts of light filtering through the window. She turned the envelope over in her hands, her fingers tracing the neat strokes of Eli's name. The memory of his warm smile surfaced, but it felt like a phantom—the connection they had shared now tangled in the web of uncertainty.

With bated breath, Esther murmured to herself, fearing the possibilities contained within the letter. "What if he's only written out of pity?" she muttered, eyes flicking toward the window as if she could glean the truth from the world outside. "Or maybe to tell me he's selling the farm to Jacob Turner after all..." The thought twisted painfully in her chest, leaving a bitter taste that hung in the back of her throat.

She clutched the envelope tightly, her heart torn between hope and dread. What could Eli possibly have to say that wouldn't make everything more complicated? He was betrothed to Martha. Their community expected him to honor that commitment. And she was here, hundreds of miles away, being courted by a kind widower who could offer her a respectable life.

Outside the door, she could hear Mary's disappointed voice: "Where did Miss Esther go? We were just getting started!"

Esther's hands shook as she stared at the sealed envelope. Inside could be anything—a simple thank you for caring for his mother, a farewell as he moved forward with his life with Martha, or... or what? What was she even hoping for?

Her mind raced with memories: the way he'd looked at her during the storm in the barn, when truth had finally broken free between them.

The weight of decision pressed down on her shoulders. She could open this letter and risk having her fragile hope shattered. Or she could preserve the small flame of possibility by not knowing, by imagining that maybe, somehow, things could have been different.

Esther turned the letter over in her hands one more time, then, in a moment of panic and self-preservation, she made a choice.

She couldn't read it. Not now. Not when she was trying so hard to accept her circumstances, to see the wisdom in choosing Aaron, to move forward instead of looking back. Reading Eli's words would only make everything harder.

Her feet carried her toward the small fireplace in the corner of the room, where embers still glowed from the morning fire. Her hand trembled as she held the envelope over the dying flames.

Just let it go, she told herself. Let him go. This is for the best. He's betrothed to Martha. You're being courted by Aaron. Reading this will only make you hurt more.

But even as she thought it, tears began streaming down her face. Because she knew—deep in her soul—that she was about to destroy something precious, something that might matter more than her fear.

"Forgive me," Esther whispered—to Eli, to herself, to *Gott*—as she released the letter into the flames.

The paper caught quickly, edges curling and blackening, Eli's careful handwriting disappearing in wisps of smoke. Esther watched, transfixed and horrified by what she'd done, as the envelope and its contents turned to ash.

She could not know that inside, Eli had poured out his heart. That he'd written of his plan to honorably end his betrothal to Martha. That he'd begged her to wait for him, to give him a chance to make things right.

She would never know that he'd written: "I've been a fool, Esther. I let pride and misunderstanding keep us apart for too long. But now I know the truth—you love me as I love you. That *Gott* wants us to be together. I'm going to find a way to fix this. Please, don't make any decisions about your future until I can speak with you properly. Wait for me."

All of it—reduced to ashes and smoke.

Esther sank onto the edge of the bed, her body shaking with silent sobs. What had she done? In trying to protect her heart, had she just destroyed her only chance at happiness?

A soft knock at the door made her jump. "Esther?" It was Hannah's gentle voice. "Are you alright? Mary is asking for you."

Esther quickly wiped her eyes, forcing her voice to steady. "I'm fine. I'll be right out."

She stood on trembling legs and moved to the small washbasin, splashing cold water on her face to hide the evidence of tears. In the mirror, her own reflection looked back at her—pale, drawn, eyes red-rimmed and haunted.

What have I done?

But there was no taking it back now. The letter was gone, its words lost forever. She would have to live with her choice, with never knowing what Eli had wanted to say to her.

Taking a deep breath, Esther smoothed her apron and straightened her *kapp*. Mary was waiting. Aaron would be home soon from his woodworking shop. Life moved forward whether she was ready or not.

As she opened the door and stepped back into the warmth of the Troyer home, Esther made herself a silent promise: she would try. She would genuinely try to see the good in this path before her, to appreciate Aaron's kindness and his *kinners'* need, to build a life here if that was what *Gott* intended.

But even as she settled back beside Mary and resumed the quilting lesson, even as she smiled and praised the little girl's improving stitches, a part of Esther's heart remained in that fireplace, burning to ash along with Eli's unread words.

* * *

That evening, as the sun painted the Ohio sky in shades of amber and rose, Esther sat in the garden with Aaron. Fireflies danced among the flowers, their gentle light weaving through the dusk like scattered stars. It should have been peaceful, romantic even. But Esther felt only a hollow numbness.

Aaron fidgeted beside her on the weathered wooden bench, the nervous energy palpable in the way he straightened his shoulders, as if summoning courage for something difficult.

"Esther," he began, his voice catching slightly, "I've been thinking about you and the time we've spent together since you arrived. I—I would like to discuss something important with you."

Esther's stomach tightened. She knew what was coming. She'd seen it building in Aaron's increasingly warm glances, in the way his children had begun calling her 'Miss Esther' with hopeful familiarity.

"I appreciate your kindness, Aaron," she replied carefully, her words measured. "You've been so welcoming."

"I know this may seem sudden," Aaron continued, "but I've thought about it carefully, prayed about it. I believe you would be a wonderful mother to my children, a good partner to help me manage the household." He paused, then added quietly, "I know this isn't a love match—not yet, anyway. But I believe love can grow between us, given time."

Esther felt tears prick her eyes, though whether from

sadness or guilt or exhaustion, she couldn't say. Aaron was offering her everything she should want—security, purpose, a family to care for. Why did it feel like settling for crumbs when she was starving for bread?

Aaron reached for a small wooden box resting in his lap, the polished surface reflecting the glimmering light of dusk. "I made this for you," he said, presenting it to her with a tentative smile.

Esther took the box with trembling hands, its weight pressing against her palms like the weight of expectation. Inside, nestled on soft fabric, lay a delicate handkerchief—freshly embroidered with her initials in careful, graceful script.

"Mary helped with the embroidery," Aaron explained, pride evident in his voice. "She wanted to contribute something personal."

The thoughtfulness of the gesture pierced through Esther's numbness. This was real—Mary's hope, Joseph's need, Aaron's genuine desire for a partner. These were real people who would be hurt by her indecision, by the love she still carried for a man she could never have.

"It's beautiful," Esther whispered, and she meant it. "Thank you, Aaron. And please thank Mary for me."

"Esther," Aaron said gently, "I'm not asking for an answer tonight. I know you need time to think, to pray about this. But I want you to know—I would be honored if you would consider becoming my wife, becoming a mother to my children."

Before Esther could respond, movement at the kitchen window caught her eye. Joseph stood there, his small face pressed against the glass, watching them with an expression of such naked hope that it made Esther's throat tighten. The little boy had lost his mother. He was looking at Esther like she might fill that terrible void in his life.

But I can't fill it, Esther thought desperately. *Not when my own heart is empty. Not when I'm still in love with someone else.*

"I'll think about it," Esther heard herself say. "And pray about it. You deserve an honest answer, Aaron, not a hasty one."

"That's all I ask," Aaron replied, relief evident in his features. He reached out as if to take her hand, then thought better of it, pulling back with appropriate restraint. "Take all the time you need."

But even as he said it, Esther felt the invisible pressure—from her aunt's expectations, from her father's concerns about her reputation, from the very real needs of two motherless children. Time was not unlimited. Eventually, she would have to choose.

As the fireflies continued their dance and the stars began emerging overhead, Esther sat in that Ohio garden and felt more lost than she'd ever been. She'd burned Eli's letter, destroyed whatever he'd wanted to tell her. She'd closed that door herself, made the choice to cut that thread.

So why did it feel like she was bleeding out from a wound that would never heal?

* * *

The next morning brought an unexpected visitor. Esther was in the kitchen helping Hannah prepare breakfast when she heard the sound of a buggy arriving. Through the window, she saw a familiar face climbing down—her sister Mae, windblown and grinning, eyes sparkling with news.

"Mae!" Esther exclaimed, rushing to the door. "What are you doing here? How did you—"

"Aunt Rebecca brought me," Mae said, practically bouncing with excitement as she swept into the house. "She was coming anyway to see someone or other here, so

I begged to tag along to see you." She paused, her face breaking into a grin. "It was some train ride! I've sure missed you."

"I've missed you too, *schwester!*"

Mae grabbed Esther's hands, squeezing tight. "Oh, Esther, you won't believe what's happened!"

Esther's heart began to race. "What? Is everyone alright? Is Mammi Yoder—"

"Everyone's fine," Mae assured her quickly. "Better than fine. Esther, Eli Yoder stood up at the community meeting. He refused Jacob Turner's offer for the farm!"

Esther felt the room tilt. "What?"

"He said—and I'm quoting him exactly because everyone's been talking about nothing else—he said: 'My family's legacy and the Amish way of life are not for sale. I'd rather lose this farm to honest debt than sell my soul to development that will destroy our community.'" Mae's eyes shone with admiration. "Oh Esther, you should have seen him. He was magnificent. Even *datt* and the bishop looked moved."

Esther sank into a chair, her mind reeling. Eli had refused the offer. He'd chosen his heritage over financial security, principle over practicality. Everything she'd accused him of being willing to betray—he'd stood up and defended.

"There's more," Mae continued, lowering her voice and glancing toward the doorway to make sure they were alone. "Martha Stoltzfus broke their betrothal."

The words didn't make sense. Esther stared at her sister, certain she'd misheard. "What?"

"She ended it," Mae confirmed, her expression growing more serious. "Apparently she marched right up to Eli after the meeting and told him she couldn't marry a man whose heart belonged to someone else. She said—and people overheard this part—she said she deserved a husband who loved her, not one who was just doing his duty."

Esther couldn't breathe. The room seemed to spin around her, Mae's words echoing in her ears like bells she couldn't quite believe were real.

"But folks say it's because she wanted the money from the farm sale, and her father's farm sale that was riding on the deal, and she didn't want to be with someone poor and that's the real reason she broke it off, but anyway, he's *free*, Esther," Mae said softly, kneeling beside her sister's chair and taking her hands. "Eli Yoder is free. And from what I've heard—from what everyone's seen—he's been a man on a mission. He's working day and night to find a way to keep the farm, talking to other farmers about combining resources, even reaching out to that new farming cooperative in Hope Valley."

"But the debts—" Esther started.

"Are still real," Mae acknowledged. "But Eli's finding solutions that don't involve selling out. He's fighting, Esther. He's fighting for everything—his land, his heritage, his future." She paused meaningfully. "And I think he's fighting for you, too."

Esther thought of the letter she'd burned, the words she would never read. Had it contained this news?

"I burned his letter," Esther whispered, horror washing over her anew. "Mae, he sent me a letter and I burned it. I didn't even read it."

Mae's eyes widened. "Oh, Esther. Why would you—"

"I was afraid," Esther confessed, tears spilling over. "Afraid it would just make everything hurt worse. Afraid he was saying goodbye, or asking me to be happy for him and Martha. I thought burning it would help me move on, help me accept—" She gestured helplessly around the Troyer kitchen. "Accept this life here."

"But you don't want this life," Mae said gently. It wasn't a question.

Esther looked at her sister through tear-blurred eyes. "Aaron is such a *gut* man. He's handsome too. Just I don't see him that way. His children need a mother. And Eli was betrothed when I left. I thought I was doing the right thing, the wise thing—"

"The safe thing," Mae corrected. "But Esther, when have you ever chosen safety over your heart?" She squeezed her sister's hands. "You need to come home. You need to talk to Eli. Whatever was in that letter, whatever he wanted to say—he deserves the chance to say it to your face."

"But Aaron—"

"Will understand," Mae said firmly. "And if he doesn't, then he's not the man you thought he was. Esther, you can't marry someone out of guilt or obligation. You can't build a life on what you think you should want instead of what you actually want."

"What if it's too late?" Esther whispered. "What if I've ruined everything?"

Mae snorted as if to say 'as if!'

Through the doorway, Esther could see Mary setting the table for breakfast, her small face serious with concentration as she arranged the plates just so. In the yard, Joseph was helping his father carry wood, his thin arms straining with the effort to be helpful, to be good enough that maybe the nice lady would stay.

They were good children. They deserved a mother who could love their father fully, not someone whose heart was perpetually elsewhere.

And Aaron deserved a wife who chose him freely, not one who settled for him because the man she really loved seemed out of reach.

Esther wiped her eyes and straightening her shoulders. She'd spent so long trying to do the wise thing, the practical thing, the thing that would protect her heart from more pain but she knew one thing with absolute certainty: she had to try. She owed it to Eli, to herself, and *ja*, even to Aaron and his children—to be honest about where her heart truly belonged.

As the morning sun streamed through the kitchen window, illuminating the domestic scene before her, Esther knew it was time to go home.

Chapter 11
The Return

Esther knelt beside the bed, the quilted square resting in her hands like a soft promise. Sunlight filtered through the window, casting a gentle glow upon the rich patterns of fabric scattered about the room. Mary sat cross-legged on the bed, her wide eyes mirroring the innocence of childhood curiosity. As Esther wrapped the square in brown paper, the weight of her own memories and the swirling uncertainty of her heart danced just beneath the surface, beckoning her to find solace in the quiet connection forming between them.

"This pattern," Esther said softly, folding the corners with care, "represents stars. They guide travelers home, just like we've been on our own journeys." She carefully tightened the string around the package, picturing those twinkling lights illuminating the path ahead—the path that would take her back to Miracle Creek, back to the life she'd almost convinced herself to leave behind.

Mary's eyes lit up, excitement bubbling beneath her skin. "Stars? Like the ones that shine at night?" Her small fingers grasped the edge of the quilt, smoothing the fabric with a reverence that tugged at Esther's heart.

"*Ja!* Just like those stars," Esther affirmed, a bittersweet smile breaking free as she watched the girl's face glow with wonder. "And you can practice making your own stars, too. I'll send you some patterns to follow." She tucked several paper templates into Mary's apron pocket, each crinkled paper a whisper of her encouragement, hoping they would ignite the same passion for quilting she had always held dear.

"Promise?" Mary asked, her eyes gleaming with sincerity, small hands clasped tightly around the folded package as if it were a treasure.

"Promise," Esther replied, and the assurance felt heavier than she'd intended, weighted with the knowledge of what she was about to do—the conversation she needed to have with Aaron, the journey home she needed to make.

Mary traced an imaginary stitch in the air with her finger, brow furrowing in concentration as she attempted to absorb Esther's instruction. "I want to make the best quilt ever!" The fervor in her voice, brimming with innocent determination, wrapped around Esther's heart.

"You will," Esther said gently, adjusting the fabric in Mary's small hands. "With practice and patience, you'll create many beautiful things." She paused, then added quietly, "Just remember that sometimes the most beautiful things come from following where your heart truly leads you, even when it's difficult."

Mary tilted her head, not quite understanding the deeper meaning but sensing something important in Esther's tone. "Are you going somewhere, Miss Esther?"

Esther's throat tightened. She'd been dreading this conversation, knowing how it would disappoint these children who had already lost so much. "I need to go home to Lancaster County," she said carefully.

"But you'll come back, won't you?" Mary's voice rose with worry.

"I'll send you patterns," Esther promised, gathering the little girl into a gentle hug. "And I'll write to you. But Mary, you need to know—your father is a really good man, but he deserves someone who can love him with her whole heart. I am not that person."

Mary pulled back, her young face suddenly older, wiser than her years. "You love someone else," she said simply. "Like in the stories Mama used to tell me about people who belonged together."

Esther blinked back tears. "*Ja,*" she whispered. "I do."

"Then you should go," Mary said with the straightforward logic of childhood.

The simple wisdom pierced Esther's heart. She kissed Mary's forehead, then rose to face the harder conversation ahead.

***

Aaron stood in his woodworking shop, running his hand over the smooth surface of the hope chest he'd been building for Mary. The smell of fresh-cut wood and linseed oil filled the air, usually bringing him peace. But today, as he watched Esther approach through the window, he felt only a heavy inevitability.

He'd known, really. From the first day she'd arrived with that distant look in her eyes, the way she smiled but never quite seemed fully present. He'd hoped that time and his children's affection might change things, might help her settle into the life he was offering. But hope wasn't the same as truth.

"Aaron," Esther said softly as she entered the workshop. "We need to talk."

He set down his plane, brushing sawdust from his hands. "I know what you're going to say."

Esther's eyes widened in surprise. "You do?"

"Your heart isn't here," Aaron said gently, gesturing to the space between them. "It never has been. I've watched you these past weeks—you're kind to my children, you help with the household, you do everything right. But you're not fully here. Part of you is always somewhere else."

Tears slipped down Esther's cheeks. "I'm so sorry, Aaron. You've been nothing but good to me. You and your children deserve so much more than—"

"Than someone who's in love with another man?"

Aaron finished, a sad smile touching his lips. "Esther, I married for love once. My late wife and I—we chose each other freely, with our whole hearts. I know what real love looks like, and I know what settling looks like too."

He moved closer, his expression kind despite the disappointment in his eyes. "I won't lie and say I'm not disappointed. I'd hoped we might build something together. But I won't trap you in a marriage where you'll always be looking back at what you left behind."

"Your children—" Esther started.

"Will be fine," Aaron assured her. "They're resilient. Go with my blessing and my hope that you find what you're looking for. And Esther—if it doesn't work out, if you need a friend or a safe place, you're always welcome here. Not as a potential wife, but as someone I've come to respect and care for."

The kindness in his offer made Esther's tears flow harder. She stepped forward and embraced him briefly, properly. "Thank you, Aaron. For understanding. For being so gracious. I pray *Gott* sends you someone who can love you and your children the way you all deserve."

"And I pray He grants you the courage to fight for your heart's desire," Aaron replied. "Now go."

* * *

The wheels of the family wagon creaked against the rugged terrain at the foot of Hope Valley, the sound mingling with the low whinnies of the horses as they pulled steadily forward. The sun began to dip toward the horizon, casting a golden glow over the fields that stretched like an endless tapestry, weaving the memories of Ohio with the promise of what lay ahead in Miracle Creek

Esther sat beside her father, his weathered hands guiding the reins with practiced ease, while she leaned forward slightly, drawn by the flickering images of home that beckoned from the road ahead.

"Look at that crooked oak tree!" Daniel exclaimed, gesturing toward a familiar landmark that stood resolutely at Miller's Crossing. Its sturdy branches swayed softly in the evening breeze, a sentinel bearing witness to the passage of time. Esther's heart swelled with recognition, the gnarled roots anchoring her memories of childhood games, whispered secrets shared beneath its expansive shade.

"Do you remember the day we played hide-and-seek there?" Esther asked Mae, her voice tinged with nostalgia as the recollection brought a smile to her father's face.

"I remember," her *datt* chuckled, eyes crinkling with fondness. "You always thought you could hide in plain sight by standing perfectly still behind that trunk."

"I thought I was invisible!" she retorted playfully, but her laughter faded as they moved on, the feelings within her shifting, anticipation coiling tighter with each familiar landmark.

Mae, sitting in the back of the wagon, leaned forward. "We're almost home, Esther. Are you nervous?"

Esther nodded, unable to find words for the tumult of emotions churning within her. What would she find when they arrived? Did Eli still want her after she'd burned his letter without reading it? Had too much time passed, too many misunderstandings accumulated?

"Whatever happens," Daniel said quietly, his eyes on the road ahead, "you've made the right choice in coming home to face it honestly. Running away—even to a *gut* situation like Aaron—is never the answer when your heart is pulling you in another direction."

As they turned onto a side road leading past the covered bridge, memories flooded Esther's mind with bittersweet intensity. This was where she and Eli had played as children, where they'd carved their initials in the wooden beams during a picnic when they were twelve—a moment of childish boldness that she'd treasured in secret for years. That was the day she first knew she loved him.

The weathered red paint of the bridge, chipped and faded, still held a certain charm, a testament to endurance through time and weather. The sight of it brought tears to her eyes, an involuntary response as the realization hit her that her heart had been pointing toward home—toward Eli—all along.

Her fingers smoothed the fabric of her apron anxiously, each pulse of her heart echoing with anticipation and dread in equal measure. What would she say to Eli when she saw him? How would she explain burning his letter? Would he understand, or would he see it as another rejection, another sign that they were meant to be apart?

As the sun began its descent, painting the sky in brilliant shades of orange and gold, Esther felt the weight of her past and future coalesce. The journey from Ohio had been more than miles traveled—it had been a journey of the heart, from fear toward courage, from resignation toward hope.

"Almost there," Daniel said softly as the familiar outline of the Troyer homestead appeared on the horizon. But Esther's eyes were already scanning the surrounding landscape.

As the wagon crested the last rise before home, Esther's breath caught. There, beside the roadside, stood a solitary figure—tall and broad-shouldered, with a familiar posture that made her heart recognize him before her eyes fully registered the details.

Eli Yoder.

Had her father mentioned to Eli she was coming back? If her father knew, he was saying nothing.

As the wagon approached, Eli stepped forward, and their eyes met across the diminishing distance. Esther saw in his face a reflection of her own tumultuous emotions— hope, fear, longing, and something that looked like desperate determination.

Daniel slowed the wagon, understanding without words that this moment belonged to Esther and Eli alone.

"Go on, *dochder,*" he said quietly. "We'll wait for you at home."

With trembling hands, Esther climbed down from the wagon, her feet touching the familiar earth of Lancaster County. Behind her, she heard the wagon moving on, leaving her standing in the golden evening light, facing the man who had haunted her dreams and prayers for almost as long as she could remember.

And as the distance between them closed—one step, then another—Esther felt the last of her fear fall away, replaced by a certainty that sang in her bones:

She was finally, truly home.

Chapter 12
A Joyful Union

Esther stood on the dusty road, the evening sun casting long shadows across the Pennsylvania countryside, her heart thundering so loudly she was certain Eli could hear it.

He took a step toward her, then another, closing the distance between them with the careful deliberation of someone approaching something precious and fragile.

"You came back," Eli said, his voice rough with emotion. "I wasn't sure—after I didn't hear from you—I thought maybe you'd decided to stay in Ohio."

"I almost did," Esther admitted, her own voice barely above a whisper. "The kids made it so hard. I was so afraid, Eli. Afraid of more heartbreak, afraid of more misunderstanding. Afraid that whatever you'd written in your letter would only make everything hurt worse."

Eli's brow furrowed. "My letter? Didn't you read it then?"

She felt heat flood her cheeks, shame and regret warring within her. Her voice broke. "I burned it. I was trying to protect my heart, trying to move forward, and I thought if I didn't read your words, it would be easier to accept Aaron."

She watched the impact of her confession wash over Eli's face—surprise, hurt, and then something that looked almost like understanding.

"You burned it," he repeated slowly.

"I'm so sorry," Esther said, tears slipping down her cheeks. "Mae told me what I guess you wrote me—she told me you're free from Martha, that you refused Jacob Turner's offer."

Eli was silent for a long moment, and Esther felt her

heart sink. She'd come all this way, turned down a good man's proposal, only to discover that she'd hurt Eli one too many times, made one too many mistakes.

He took another step closer, and now they stood mere feet apart, the golden light of sunset wrapping around them like a blessing.

"The truth that I love you," Eli said, his voice steady and sure. "That I've loved you since we were children. That I accepted my father's idea of the betrothal to Martha because I thought you didn't want me, and I was trying to do the practical thing, the honorable thing. But there's no honor in marrying someone when your heart belongs to another."

"Martha," Esther breathed. "Is she—"

"She's fine," Eli assured her quickly. "Better than fine, actually. She's already being courted by Veronica Zook's nephew, and from what I've seen, they're much better suited than she and I ever were." He paused, a slight smile touching his lips. Melvin Zook had a large property.

Esther's heart felt too large for her chest, hope blooming like spring flowers after a long winter.

"The farm's debts are being managed," Eli said gently. "I've partnered with three other farmers to create a cooperative. We're sharing equipment, combining resources, helping each other through the difficult seasons. It won't be easy, Esther. We'll have lean years ahead. But we'll keep our land, our heritage, our community intact."

He reached out tentatively, and Esther found her own hand moving to meet his, their fingers intertwining like the threads of a well-made quilt—separate strands woven together to create something stronger than either could be alone.

"I can't offer you an easy life," Eli said, his eyes searching hers. "I can't promise wealth or financial certainty. But I can promise you I love you."

"I don't want an easy life," Esther replied, her voice strengthening with conviction. "I want a true one. A life built on love and faith and the courage to choose each other, even when it's difficult. Especially when it's difficult."

Eli's thumb brushed across her knuckles, the simple touch sending warmth flooding through her. "Then will you—can you forgive me for the wasted years? For believing your denial instead of trusting what I felt between us? For almost letting pride and misunderstanding destroy our chance at happiness?"

"Only if you'll forgive me," Esther said. "For denying my feelings out of embarrassment. For burning your letter without reading it. For being too afraid to fight for what we both wanted."

"Consider it done," Eli said, and the smile that broke across his face was like sunrise after the darkest night. "Esther Troyer, I'm standing before you now, in full daylight, with the whole community likely watching from their windows, and I'm telling you the plain truth: I love you. I've always loved you. And if you'll have me—if you'll take a farmer with debts and dreams and a mother who's already planning our wedding—I'd like to court you properly. To do this right, the way we should have done it years ago."

Esther laughed through her tears, joy and relief cascading through her like a waterfall. "Eli Yoder, I'd like nothing more."

And there, on that dusty country road with the sunset painting the sky in shades of promise, Eli leaned down and Esther rose up, and their lips met in a kiss that was tentative and tender and absolutely perfect—a first kiss that was also a homecoming, an ending that was truly a beginning.

When they finally pulled apart, both breathless and grinning like fools, Esther noticed movement from the nearby farmhouses. Curtains twitching, faces peering out, the unmistakable sign of a community that had been watching and waiting and hoping for exactly this moment.

"I think we have an audience," Esther whispered, cheeks flushing.

"Let them watch," Eli said, his arm moving around her waist with protective tenderness. "I'm done hiding how I feel about you. I'm done pretending that duty matters more than love."

From down the road, Esther heard a familiar whoop of joy—Mae, no doubt, celebrating from the Troyer farmhouse. And from Eli's property, she could just make out Mammi Yoder standing on the porch, a handkerchief pressed to her eyes, shoulders shaking with what looked like happy tears.

"Your grandmother," Esther said, sudden worry creeping in. "Will she approve? Does she think I'm—"

"She adores you," Eli interrupted. "She's been pestering me daily about when I was going to 'stop being foolish and go after that Troyer girl before she marries someone else.' Her words, not mine." He grinned. "I think she's already planned our entire wedding, including the menu."

Esther laughed, then sobered slightly. "There will be talk, you know. About the broken betrothal, about us courting so soon after, about—"

"Let folks talk," Eli said firmly. "We know the truth. Gott, our judge, knows the truth."

He paused, his expression growing more serious. "We'll have to work hard, live simply, trust in *Gott's* provision."

"I know," Esther said simply. "And I choose the life anyway because I choose you, Eli, rich or poor. I choose us. I choose the hard work and the simple life and *ja*, even the wagging tongues and judgment. Because I've seen what the alternative looks like—and that's not living at all."

Eli's eyes shone with unshed tears. "When did you become so wise?"

"When I almost lost you," Esther admitted. "When I sat by a creek in Ohio and prayed for *Gott* to either take away the pain or show me a path forward. He chose to show me the path—and it led straight back to you."

As the last rays of sunlight painted the sky in brilliant rose and gold, Eli took both of Esther's hands in his. "Then let's walk that path together. One step at a time, one day at a time, trusting that the *Gott* who brought us through the wilderness of misunderstanding will guide us through whatever comes next."

"Together," Esther agreed, the word a promise and a prayer.

And there, surrounded by the fields that had witnessed their childhood games and teenage longings, their adult heartbreaks and finally their hard-won love, Esther and Eli stood hand in hand as darkness fell—no longer two hearts yearning across impossible distances, but two souls finally, irrevocably home.

* * *

The following spring, the gathering house overflowed with community members who had come to witness the marriage of Eli Yoder and Esther Troyer. The morning sun streamed through the tall windows, illuminating the scene in soft golden light, as if nature herself blessed this long-delayed union.

Esther stood at the front of the room, her wedding dress a simple but beautifully crafted deep blue—the color of summer skies and endless possibilities. Her fingers trembled slightly as she smoothed the fabric, feeling the weight of this moment, the culmination of ten years of longing, of months of heartbreak, of weeks of joyful preparation.

Eli stood across from her, impossibly handsome in his wedding suit, his eyes never leaving her face. The love and wonder in his expression made Esther's breath catch—this was real, this was happening, this was the beginning they'd both fought so hard to reach.

Bishop Samuel Lapp stepped forward, his weathered face creased with a smile that suggested he'd known all along how this story would end.

"Dearly beloved," he began, his voice resonating through the packed room, "we gather today not only to witness a union between two souls but to celebrate the weaving of two lives, bound together through faith and love, tested by trial and proven true."

Esther caught glimpses of her loved ones in the audience—her father in the front row, pride and approval shining in his eyes; Mae barely containing her excitement; Aunt Rebecca dabbing at her eyes with a handkerchief, her earlier objections apparently forgotten in the face of obvious true love.

And there, in a place of honor, sat Mammi Yoder, fully recovered and radiant with joy, her eyes glistening as she watched her grandson marry the woman who had healed more than just her body—she'd helped heal her son's wounded heart.

Even Aaron Lapp had come all the way from Ohio with Joseph and Mary to stay with Bishop Lapp and witness this special day. There seemed to be no hard feelings—Aaron appeared genuinely delighted for the couple.

"My gosh, he's so handsome!" Deborah Peachey whispered to Emma Albrecht, her eyes fixed on Aaron. "Who is that man?"

"Bishop Lapp's kin," Emma replied with a mischievous grin. "You should go talk to him—he's looking right over at you!"

The women giggled, stealing glances at each other and at Aaron as the ceremony continued, Deborah sneaking occasional, shy looks in his direction.

"Marriage is not entered into lightly," Bishop Samuel continued, "but reverently, joyfully, and in the fear of *Gott*. It requires patience in trial, courage in uncertainty, and above all, the willingness to speak truth even when silence seems easier."

They exchanged their personal vows then—words they'd written together, sitting at Mammi Yoder's kitchen table, speaking all the truths that silence had once concealed. By the end, there wasn't a dry eye in the gathering house.

"By the power vested in me," Bishop Samuel proclaimed, "I now pronounce you husband and wife. You may kiss your bride."

Eli cupped Esther's face in his hands with infinite tenderness, and when their lips met, it was different from that first kiss on the roadside—this was a promise sealed, a covenant made, the beginning of the rest of their lives.

The congregation erupted not in applause—that wasn't their way—but in a collective sigh of satisfaction, of rightness restored, of a love story that had finally found its happy ending.

As Esther and Eli turned to face their community as husband and wife, hands clasped tightly together, Esther felt overwhelming gratitude wash over her. For the trials that had tested them, for the misunderstandings that had taught them to communicate, for the heartbreak that had shown them how precious love truly was.

"Ready?" Eli whispered, squeezing her hand.

"For anything," Esther replied, "as long as we face it together."

And as they walked down the aisle, past the smiling faces of family and friends, past the obstacles they'd overcome and toward the uncertain but bright future ahead, Esther knew with absolute certainty that every tear, every prayer, every moment of doubt had been worth it.

They had found their way home—to each other, to themselves, to the love that had been waiting all along, patient and persistent as the turning of seasons, inevitable as sunrise after the darkest night.

* * *

The celebration that followed was everything a wedding feast should be—joyful, abundant, and full of love. The open-sided pavilion had been decorated with wildflowers, and long tables groaned under the weight of roasted chicken, fresh bread, potato salad, and pies of every variety.

As Esther and Eli took their seats at the head table, Daniel Troyer rose to offer a blessing and a gift. His voice carried across the gathering, strong and sure.

"I've watched these two young people grow up," Daniel began, "and I've seen the connection between them from the time they were children. It hasn't always been an easy path—sometimes *Gott* tests us, shapes us, prepares us for the blessings He has in store. But I believe Eli and Esther's love is stronger now for having been tested."

He pulled out a rolled document, and Esther's breath caught as she recognized what it was.

"This is the deed to a plot of land," Daniel continued, "It's yours—my gift to your marriage, and my blessing on your union. May you build your life together on solid ground, in every sense."

Esther felt tears stream down her face as Eli stood to accept the deed, gripping her father's hand in a firm shake that spoke of respect, gratitude, and the forging of family bonds.

The gifts continued—quilts from the women's circle, tools from the men, offers of help with building a home on their new land. The community that had watched and worried and sometimes judged was now surrounding them with support, demonstrating that at their best, they were truly a people who cared for their own.

* * *

As the stars began emerging overhead, painting the Pennsylvania sky with points of light that had witnessed their whole story—the childhood games, the teenage longings, the adult heartbreaks, and finally this perfect moment of promise—Eli and Esther stood in the doorway of their new beginning.

Behind them, laughter and music drifted from the wedding feast. Around them, the fields whispered with growing things, with potential, with life waiting to unfold. And ahead of them stretched a future uncertain in its details but absolutely certain in its foundation: love, faith, and the courage to choose each other every single day.

They stood together in comfortable silence, wrapped in each other's arms, until a voice called from across the field —Mae, no doubt, sent to fetch them back to the celebration.

"We should go back," Esther said reluctantly.

"In a moment," Eli replied, holding her closer. "Let me have just one more moment of this—my wife, our life ahead of us. Let me hold onto this perfect moment before we go back to the beautiful chaos of reality."

Esther smiled against his chest, feeling the steady beat of his heart beneath her cheek. And as they finally turned to walk back toward their wedding feast, toward the community that had shaped them and would surround their family, toward all the joys and challenges that marriage and parenthood and life itself would bring—Esther knew that their story had finally found its true beginning.

Some loves are worth waiting for. Some loves are worth fighting for. And some loves—the truest ones—are worth every tear, every prayer, every moment of doubt that leads finally, inevitably, joyfully home.

Other books in Miracle Creek series:

Each Book Can Be Read Standalone.

Out now!

THE AMISH DOCTOR'S BRIDE - BOOK 1
ISBN 978-1-918219-13-5

*She has followed the rules of her Amish faith her entire life—
until the day she assists intriguing Englisch physician.
His modern medicine saves lives… but his touch ignites a
forbidden yearning she cannot deny.*

THE AMISH CARPENTER'S HEART - BOOK 2
ISBN 978-1-918219-15-9

*She thought her prayers had gone unanswered.
God was just waiting to give her more than she'd dreamed.*

HEARTS IN THE SNOW - BOOK 3
ISBN 978-1918219234

*He left the Amish world years ago...
This Christmas, he's coming home—
for the woman he never forgot.*